To Marga

FULL CIRCLE

by

Valerie M. Walland

Valerie M Walland

Silverdale Books

Full Circle

ISBN 0-9539567-2-5

Published by Silverdale Books
42 West Malvern Road
Malvern
WR14 4NA

Design & production co-ordinated by:
The Better Book Company Ltd
Hampshire PO9 2XH
+44[0]2392 481160

Printed in England.

Cover design by Dudley Brook

Asking nothing and giving much in return
looking for no reward, save a smile
and laughter's ever-present magic

Needing no flattery or false reassurance
where none is offered

Here is a friendship, an acceptance
in all ways good, true and rare
touching all life's corners and
ending the dark loneliness.

"FRIENDSHIP" by RUTH WALLAND

Other works by the same author:

Ever Whirling Wheels

Marcus

CHAPTER ONE

LONDON – 1885

The telephone jangled. Removing the receiver from its rest she placed it firmly against her ear and, speaking loudly and clearly into the mouthpiece, said

"London Six – Douglass & Co."

A tinny voice instructed

"Go ahead, caller."

After a slight pause a distorted female voice asked

"Is that you, Amelia?"

"Yes."

"Patience Douglass here. Is Arthur with you?"

"No, I'm afraid not, Mrs Douglass. I haven't seen him since this morning. Anything I can do?"

"I need him." Mrs Douglass sounded tearful. "It's Eleanor, you see. She's locked herself in her room again and Arthur is the only one that can make her come out."

"If I see him I'll ask him to telephone you."

"Thank you, dear."

Amelia replaced the receiver with a sigh. Poor Arthur. He had probably escaped down the factory to look at his beloved machines. Life had not been easy for him. First his only child, Eleanor, had made an unhappy marriage from which she was only released when her husband was murdered and now it seemed she was becoming more and more deranged.

Going into Arthur's room she discovered Miss Prentice, the Typewriter, in the act of covering her machine preparatory to going home.

"Where is Mr Douglass, Miss Prentice?"

"He has just left, Miss Wallace. He didn't say where he was going."

"Thank you, Miss Prentice. Good night."

"Good night, Miss Wallace."

Walking back into her office, she glanced at the small pendant watch which was pinned to her crisp, white blouse. It was later than she had realized and she knew that Bert would be waiting with the cab. Retrieving her cloak and bonnet from the coatstand she hastily put them on. As she tied her bonnet strings she debated whether to take her half-completed design home and finish it after dinner. She was very tired but if she did not finish the design soon it would be too late to produce the toy for the Christmas trade. Making up her mind, she picked up her handbag from the desk, thrust the pad inside, left the room and walked down the corridor to the main office. As she entered the room, Mr. Higgins, the Chief Clerk, looked up from his desk and smiled.

"Goodnight, Miss Wallace."

"Goodnight, Mr Higgins. Oh, do you know where Mr Douglass is? Mrs Douglass has just telephoned to say she needs him at home, urgently."

"He went home a few minutes ago. Would you like me to telephone Mrs Douglass and let her know he is on his way?"

"Thank you, Mr Higgins, that would be most helpful."

As Amelia made her way down the long room past clerks at their desks industriously scribbling in large ledgers she reflected how, when the telephone was first installed, Mr Higgins had announced his intention of having nothing whatsoever to do with it. It had taken one murder and an attempted murder to make him change his mind.

When she got to the factory gates she found the hansom waiting. She always had the same cabby and over the years she had got used to conversing with Bert's upside down face as he peered down through the trap door in the roof of the cab to tell her about the vagaries of his life as a cabby, the difficulties of putting food into the mouths of an increasing family, the high price of stabling and feed for his horse and how he would rather be out in the country on a little farm away from London. Tonight she only half listened as he gave her an account of a disagreement he had had with a fare which was only resolved after the intervention of a Policeman. She was worried about Arthur. It was unusual for him to leave the building without saying goodnight. He had been very preoccupied lately.

"I said we're 'ere, Miss – Springfield Road."

Amelia woke with a start.

"Sorry Bert. I'm tired."

"Well you go to bed early. My Missus swears by a good night's sleep. Always anaggin' me about it she is."

"She's probably right." Amelia agreed as she descended from the cab.

"Thank you, Bert. I'll see you in the morning."

"I'll be 'ere 8.30 on the dot."

Bert slapped the reins on the horse's back and the cab moved off down the street, Bert touching the brim of his bowler with his whip handle in farewell.

Amelia rang the front door bell and was surprised when it was answered by her friend Rose rather than Ethel, their housemaid.

"Where's Ethel?" she asked as she hung her cloak and bonnet on the hallstand.

"Ethel has left." Rose replied, crisply.

"Left! Why?"

"She has decided to get married and insisted on leaving today without working out her notice."

"And Aunt Isabella let her?"

"You know how soft Madam is with servants. Ethel burst into tears and Madam gave in straight away. Now we are without a housemaid."

"But we still have a cook?"

"Oh yes, Mrs Gipps is still with us but it's not the same as having a servant living in. Still, I expect we shall manage."

"I am so sorry, Rose. I will help you, of course."

"And so will I."

Mrs Trevise had come out into the hall.

"After all, it is my fault."

"How can it be your fault, Aunt Isabella?"

"I should have realised how unreliable Ethel was."

"Her dusting was very inefficient." Rose sniffed.

Amelia hid a smile. Rose was always very critical of other people's dusting.

Later that evening, half-dozing by the fire, Amelia idly watched Rose and Aunt Isabella as they searched through the newspaper advertisements for Domestic Agencies. Aunt Isabella's hair was now completely white. She wondered how old she was, probably near her mother's age she thought. Rose was still a very striking looking woman with her black hair and green eyes. She came out of her reverie to hear Rose saying

"You must go to a reputable Agency, Madam. Otherwise you will be taking on the first girl that gives you a hard-luck story."

"I feel so sorry for them, Rose They are paid such poor wages. I wish I could give them more."

Rose was shocked.

"I really don't think that is a very good idea, Madam. They would only get ideas above their station and waste it on bonnets and such fripperies."

"Did you waste your money on bonnets and fripperies, Rose." Amelia asked, mischievously.

"No, I did not!" Rose replied, indignantly.

Mrs Trevise swiftly intervened before Amelia could make one of her devastating comments.

"I think, Rose, that I will ask you to conduct the interviews, then we can be sure of getting a satisfactory girl."

After some discussion it was agreed that Mrs Trevise would go to the selected Domestic Agency the next day and see if there was a suitable candidate. She would then make arrangements for the girl to come and be interviewed by Rose.

Mrs Trevise cleared her throat which Amelia knew was a prelude to her saying something she had been steeling herself up to for days.

"I wish we could be on a less formal footing, Rose. With Amelia out all day it would have been very lonely for me if you had not been here especially as Selina still refuses to speak to me."

"I'm sure she will come round one day, Aunt Isabella. You are her mother, nothing can alter that."

"But it has been so long, Amelia. I went round to No 13 again this morning. There was yet another new servant and I hoped this time Selina would see me but, when I gave the servant my name, she said what they always say 'Mrs Wallace has given strict instructions that you are not to be admitted' then she slammed the door in my face!"

Mrs Trevise's voice trembled then she cleared her throat and continued.

"What do you say to my proposal, Rose?"

Rose shook her head.

"I'm sorry, Madam, but it would not feel right. I would prefer things to stay as they are. Could I suggest that you call me your Housekeeper – after all, that is what I am."

Mrs Trevise brightened at this suggestion.

"Very well, Rose, if that is what you wish."

She paused

"There is something else that I feel I must say, Rose. We have just drifted along all these years and you have looked after us and managed the house with only a small allowance in return. I know your one thought has been to stay with Amelia but as my Central Argentine Railway Shares are doing very well at the moment I can afford to pay you a larger allowance – perhaps double?"

Rose looked as if she was about to protest but, seeing Amelia give a slight shake of the head, replied

"Thank you, Madam. That would be very satisfactory. I could buy more books!"

"You and your books, Rose. You must have more books in your room than they have in the Circulating Library!"

Amelia laughed.

"So long as I can stay here with Amelia until she doesn't need me any more."

"That time will never come!" Amelia stated, firmly.

"That's settled then." Mrs Trevise beamed, "and of course you can stay here as long as you like, Rose, this is your home."

"I do feel at home here. Thank you, Madam."

Later, as they were lighting their candles preparatory to retiring for the night, Amelia asked

"Are you happy here, Rose? Have you never wanted to get married again?"

"No, Amelia. Of course, I shall never forget George or the baby but it is a long time ago and I am very happy as I am. Now go to bed and don't spend half the night on those drawings of yours."

Amelia smiled and said

"Good night, Rose."

She would just spend a short time on the design. She thought she knew how to overcome the problem.

The design was completed just as St Mary's Church clock struck two. Her head ached and she was very tired but she felt much happier as she blew out her candle and settled down to sleep.

★★★★★

Amelia was busy all the next day and only saw Arthur in the late afternoon when he came into her office to ask how the new design was progressing. She showed him the completed design and, after they had discussed a few modifications, she remembered to ask him if he had received Mrs Douglass's message the day before.

"Yes, I arrived home just as Higgins telephoned. Patience was hysterical. I don't know what I am going to do about Eleanor, Amelia, she seems to exist in a world of her own. Patience doesn't seem able to get through to her and I don't know how much longer I shall be able to do so. It's a great worry."

"I'm sorry Arthur, I only wish there was something I could do."

"There is nothing you *can* do, Amelia. I'm going to have another word with the Doctor, he might be able to suggest something."

Sighing, Arthur walked to the communicating door between their offices remarking.

"I must give Miss Prentice some dictation or she will think I've forgotten her."

The rest of the afternoon flew by and soon Amelia was ringing the front door bell and wondering as she did so if Aunt Isabella had managed to engage a servant. She hoped they would find one before Christmas otherwise her Aunt would be in a fever of anxiety.

The front door was opened by Rose and Amelia's heart sank. Rose had her 'I am very annoyed but I am not going to say anything' look. Amelia waited as she knew from experience that her friend would be unable to keep her grievance to herself. Sure enough, once Amelia had removed her cloak and bonnet, Rose followed her into the drawing room and, after enquiring whether Amelia would like some tea, said

"Although whether we shall get tea or something entirely different remains to be seen."

Amelia waited.

"I am very fond of Madam but sometimes… ."

She shook her head.

"What has upset you, Rose? Is it something to do with the new housemaid?"

"Madam promised me faithfully she would go to the Domestic Agency and engage a suitable girl."

"Didn't she?"

"No! She did not. Apparently, she was on her way there when she found a young girl huddled in a doorway, crying. Of course Madam enquired what was the matter."

"Yes, she is very kind. What happened?"

Amelia yawned – she was so tired.

"The girl, Amy Paget, told Madam she was repairing a tear in her only dress before her Mistress saw it and scolded her or worst still, beat her. One of the children in the family saw her and told their mother that she had seen Amy sewing on a Sunday and her Mistress turned her out there and then."

"That is very harsh. I'm not surprised Aunt Isabella took her in."

Rose leaned forward in her chair

"We know nothing about her. She says she is fourteen. I had hoped Madam would engage someone more mature. When I asked Amy for the name of her previous employer so that Madam could write to her for a reference the girl had hysterics and said she would go. It took me a long time to calm her down. And then it all came out. She told me she had been in an orphanage for as long as she could remember and had no idea who her parents were. When one day she was sent for and told by the Superintendent that a charitable lady had decided to take her in and train her as a domestic servant, she was over the moon. But she found it was worse than the orphanage. She was ill-treated until finally she was turned out of the house at a moment's notice without a reference. I must admit that I feel sorry for the girl."

Rose paused for breath.

"It sounds as if the poor girl has had a dreadful life. We must give Amy a chance to prove herself. You never know, she could turn out to be a treasure – another Rose in fact!"

Amelia was pleased to see Rose smile – reluctantly, but it was still a smile which Mrs Trevise, entering the room at that moment was also relieved to see. There was no one like Amelia for sorting out domestic problems! A very small, painfully thin young girl carrying a large tea tray had followed Mrs Trevise into the room. Now she set the tray down very carefully on a table by the fire. As she straightened she caught sight of Amelia and gasped. Amelia felt a surge of irritation, would she never get used to people's reaction when they saw her face?

Rose tutted and got to her feet.

"Come along, Amy. I'll show you where everything is in the kitchen and instruct you in your duties."

She ushered the still goggling Amy out of the room.

Going over to Amelia Mrs Trevise put her arm round her.

"I'm sorry, Amelia, I didn't think to warn her. It must have been very distressing for you."

"I'm used to the stares, Aunt Isabella. Every time I go out I know I'm going to be stared at. You can't really blame people. It's not usual to have one side of your face lower than the other, is it? I can't do anything about it and I don't intend staying indoors for ever or wear a veil every time I leave the house, so people will just have to put up with it."

Seeing her Aunt look concerned she added

"Don't be upset for me, Aunt Isabella. I'm quite used to it."

"I don't think you are" Mrs Trevise thought but knew better than to express her opinion aloud. Amelia gave the impression of being reconciled to a life of spinsterhood and seemed happy doing her drawings but she had eyes, she could see other women of her own age with a husband and children, enjoying the sort of life she could never have. She hoped that Rose would never desert her. She had made provision in her will for both of them and as she had left Amelia the house she would not be homeless but she would dearly love to see Amelia married and in a home of her own. She sighed.

Misinterpreting the sigh and thinking Aunt Isabella was still worried about Rose and Amy, Amelia asked.

"Tell me how you found Amy."

Mrs Trevise gave a similar account to the one Rose had given only adding

"I think there was some trouble with the Mistress's son."

"You didn't tell Rose this?"

"I thought it best not to mention it to Rose as she would probably be convinced it was the girl's fault and might insist we turn her off.

The poor child has nowhere to go and who knows what would happen to her? Besides Rose was so cross with me that I thought it would only make things worse. I *did* promise her she would be interviewing applicants. Do you think she is very offended?"

"She is certainly not pleased but I'm sure she will get over it and she will enjoy training Amy to be a 'proper servant!'"

Mrs Trevise looked relieved.

Dinner that evening was late. As it was Mrs Gipp's, the Cook's, day off Rose decided that she would make a Brown Bread pudding, Amelia's favourite and asked Amy to fetch her three eggs from the larder. On the way back Amy dropped an egg and immediately began to repeat over and over again "break an egg break a leg". It was not until Rose took the two intact eggs from her and told her very sharply to clean up the mess that she stopped her monotonous chanting.

Over the next few days Mrs Trevise repeated to Amelia all the superstitious sayings Amy had uttered during the day. Rose was inclined to ignore it all which Amelia thought was the most sensible thing to do but, when it became clear that Mrs Trevise was beginning to wonder if there was anything in it, Amelia became irritated. Things came to a head when one evening Amelia arrived home to be let in by a furious-looking Rose.

"What has happened now, Rose?" Amelia wearily enquired as Rose helped her off with her cloak and bonnet.

Rose gave an unladylike snort.

"The stupid girl was dusting a bedroom upstairs this morning when a bumble bee flew in through an open window. She came screaming downstairs shouting that 'a bumble bee in the house means someone will never leave it alive'. Madam and Amy have been in a state ever since."

"In that case there is only one thing to be done. Where is Amy now?"

"I told her to stay in the kitchen with Mrs Gipps."

"And Aunt Isabella?"

"In the drawing room."

Amelia took her cloak down from the hallstand.

"Fetch shawls for Aunt Isabella and yourself."

"What are you going to do?"

"Settle this nonsense once and for all."

While Rose collected the woollen shawls Amelia marched to the kitchen where she found Amy sitting huddled on a kitchen chair, sobbing hysterically. Mrs Gipps, hands on ample hips, was standing over her saying

"I never heard such nonsense. Pull yourself together you *silly* girl!"

Going over to Amy, Amelia grasped her by the arm and hauled her to her feet.

"Come along, Amy. We will all go out into the garden and nobody will die."

"I dare'sn't, Miss." Amy sobbed clinging on to the chair.

"Mrs Gipps, fetch your shawls." Amelia ordered, and, picking up a lamp from the dresser lit it and waited impatiently while Mrs Gipps took two shawls from behind the kitchen door placing one round Amy's thin shoulders and wrapping herself in the other. Then they forcibly marched the sobbing Amy out into the moonlit garden where they found Rose and an apprehensive-looking Mrs Trevise.

Standing in front of the shivering women Amelia shone the lamp on each in turn as she asked

"We are all outside the house and I don't see anyone missing, do you, Amy?"

Amy's sobs died down into intermittent hiccups as she looked at each of them in turn.

"No, Miss Wallace" Amy damply replied, then brightening "but perhaps I 'ad it all wrong – per'aps a bumble bee in the 'ouse means somethin' else! What if it…"

"That is quite enough, Amy. I don't know where you get all this nonsense from but it is obviously not true about bumble bees as you can see. You didn't break a leg when you dropped the egg did you?

All this has got to stop, you are upsetting the whole household. Now, either you keep your superstitions to yourself or you will have to leave our employment."

Amy began to sob once more.

"I really don't think..." Mrs Trevise began.

"I'm sorry, Aunt Isabella, but I think it is the only way. I'm sure Amy understands that don't you, Amy?"

"Yes, Miss!" Amy sobbed.

"Good, now we can go back into the warm before we all catch our death of cold. Perhaps you would make us all a hot drink, Mrs Gipps."

"Certainly, Miss Wallace. Come along Amy, you can help me."

As they trooped back inside Rose said

"You sounded just like your dear Papa then, Amelia."

"I still miss him, Rose."

"Of course you do, so do I. He once helped me when my future was very bleak indeed. He was a kind gentleman."

Amelia would love to have known what the story was behind this remark but had no chance to pursue it.

The next day thinking to cheer Arthur up she told him about Amy and her superstitions.

"I hope that Amy keeps her superstitions to herself. I don't want to get rid of the girl, she has nowhere to go. It is so tiresome going home to all these domestic problems."

"Well, this is how it has always been. We go out into the world to earn enough money to enable the womenfolk to stay at home and run the house which works very well most of the time but as soon as there is any trouble they can't wait to tell us. We work hard all day and it's not fair to burden us with trivial domestic matters as soon as we set foot inside the house. But we must remember that the woman is the weaker vessel and cannot..."

As Amelia began to giggle he stopped, confused. They looked at each other then both collapsed in helpless laughter. Eventually Arthur blew his nose and said

"I sometimes forget you are female, Amelia. You're like the son I never had."

"Thank you, Arthur, that is nice of you. It is good to see you laughing again."

"It is good to laugh. You know it is hard to see your child suffer, at least that is something you will be spared, Amelia."

"Yes, I suppose it is." She hastily changed the subject.

"Did you manage to calm Mrs. Jarrett?"

"It took me longer than usual. Eleanor is convinced Anderson is going to come after her and kill her too. That's why she locks herself in her bedroom. I told her that he had been captured and was in prison. Did I do wrong, Amelia?"

"I don't think so. It *has* been seven years and he could well be in prison or dead by now, we have no way of knowing. What did the Doctor say?"

"He gave her a sedative. He still thinks that she will recover in time."

Amelia yawned.

"Sorry, Arthur, I'm very tired."

"You're working too hard. Don't come in tomorrow morning then you can have the whole weekend to rest."

"No, I have to finish the rest of the designs tomorrow or we will be behind."

By the time Amelia got home the next afternoon she was very tired and sneezing.

"You've caught a chill standing out in the cold garden when you were so tired."

Rose scolded as she put her to bed with a stone hot water bottle.

Amelia was still sneezing the next day so could not attend Morning Prayer at St Mary's as usual. On their return Mrs Trevise went to Amelia's room to see how she was and to give her all the news. Apparently, the Vicar had been taken ill and there was a stranger conducting the Service, the choir had been worse than usual and

Amy had become very agitated when the Church clock struck during the last hymn, but after a stern look from Rose, she had subsided to a low muttering.

"And then, just as we were coming out of Church, Rose discovered that she had lost her brooch. You know how fond she is of it."

Amelia had often admired the unusual brooch – a gold heart tendril with three pearls suspended from the centre. Rose had told her that it had been a present from her mother on the very day that Amelia was born and Rose began work as a housemaid for the Wallace family. As a special treat, when Amelia was very small Rose would take the brooch from the inside of her dress where she pinned it out of sight and let Amelia admire it. Since Rose had lived at Springfield Road and was no longer a housemaid she always wore it at the neck of her dress.

"Poor Rose she must be *so* upset."

"Well, no"

"No!" Amelia sat up in bed, sneezed and continued "But she must be! It was the last gift her mother ever gave her!"

"No, because an elderly woman came out with it in her hand! She had seen it fall to the floor. Fortunately it was not damaged but Rose will have to get the clasp mended before she wears it again. Anyway, the woman, whose name is Mrs Kitson, told us that she had just moved here from Scotland. I don't think she has any family so I thought it would be kind to invite her to tea one afternoon. Rose seemed to take to her and it would be nice to have a visitor. Of course we will wait until you are better."

Amelia gave a convulsive sneeze.

"Now you must get some sleep. If you are no better in the morning I am sending Rose for the Doctor."

"I shall be fine" Amelia protested but she was relieved when Mrs Trevise left the room enabling her to snuggle down and go to sleep.

CHAPTER TWO

In another part of London John Wallace sat brooding by the fire. He felt very lonely tonight. He bitterly regretted becoming estranged from his youngest sister. He had healed the breach between himself and his mother years before but had never managed to bring himself to approach Amelia. He wished Selina would forgive them both. She had every right to be upset but seven years was a very long time. She made no effort with anything. The servants were indolent and his wife seemed incapable of keeping them in order. The dinner this evening had been almost inedible, not that Selina would notice. She scarcely touched the food. He knew she was drinking heavily and it worried him. He remembered when he had brought her to this very house to meet his family. She had been so pretty. Now her charming plumpness was turning to ugly fat, her face, pretty no longer, wore a permanent look of discontent, the voice that once he had thought so beautifully modulated had become shrill.

This evening at dinner, almost before the servant had left the room, she had brought up, yet again, the question of when she could expect to become Lady Selina Wallace.

"Never, I should imagine." John had replied as he attempted to carve the leathery beef.

"When you asked me to marry you you said you would be knighted quite soon."

"I said no such thing. I expect I shall become a *Lord* when *you* provide me with an *heir*!" he said, spitefully.

Throwing down her napkin Selina rose from the table.

"How unkind you are. You know it is your ugly sister's fault that I cannot have children."

She began to sob, noisily. Only a year ago John would have gone to her and comforted her, now he sat and watched her. A suspicion had been growing in his mind lately that Amelia had been telling the truth seven years ago and Selina had procured an abortion.

When it became clear that John had no intention of doing anything other than finish his dinner, Selina left the room. Now he was sitting by the fire, brooding. He glanced at the marble clock on the mantelpiece. He would go to his Club; it was still early enough to get into a card game.

Going out into the hall he called for Jane, the housemaid. He called several times becoming more and more impatient as the minutes passed. Eventually she came through the heavy mahogany door that led from the hall into the kitchen quarters.

"Yes?"

"I'm going out. Fetch my outdoor things and look sharp."

Jane took her time and John was fuming as she helped him, none too gently, into his coat and handed him his hat and cane.

"I would advise you to stir yourself, Jane or you will be looking for another place."

The only reply he received was the front door banged behind him.

Fuming, he hailed a passing cab. As the cab made its way into the City he reflected that they seemed to have a new servant every week each one more insolent than the last. His mother would never have tolerated it. When she had been in charge of No. 13 everything had run like clockwork. Mrs Coalport, the cook, and Rose, the housemaid had been the perfect servants. As he felt a stab of indigestion he cursed Mrs Merryweather's cooking. He would never understand why Selina had dismissed Mrs Coalport, one of the best cooks in London. The house had not been the same since. Then his thoughts turned to his business problems. The firm was not doing well. There was more competition for automata than ever from Germany and France. That was not his fault. It was fate. Can't do anything against fate. It was not fair, everything was against him, as usual.

As he paid off the cab he felt a pang of guilt. Years ago his father had warned him against gambling, paying off his debts on condition that he left the cards alone in future. But Papa was dead and he, John, was in charge now. Anyway, he was sure he would be lucky tonight – bad luck could not go on for ever, it had to turn sometime and he was convinced that tonight was the night. Feeling more cheerful he ran up the Club steps.

Seven hours later, he slowly retraced his steps. The dawn was breaking on a crisp November morning. The sun was just rising in a clear cold blue sky, London sparrows were twittering and the air felt invigorating but to John it might just as well have been thick fog.

He had won the sum he had lost and more. Convinced he was on a winning streak, he had gambled everything on the turn of one card – and, unbelievably, had lost. He could not cover his bet and had had to write several IOU's. He had no idea how he was going to redeem them.

Unable to afford even an omnibus fare he began to walk home and as he walked he thought. He had taken all he could and more from the business. He had had a succession of designers, none of whom had the flair that his father and, yes, Amelia had and only the previous day his designer had informed him that he had decided to leave the firm and take up a position with one of the Continental toy manufacturers where there was "more appreciation for my talents in the form of remuneration." John had never liked the man but he was better than nothing. He knew his rival, Arthur Douglass, had employed Amelia and they were doing well. She should be designing for him. If only she had not caused Selina to lose the baby. His mother had believed Selina at first but, eventually, she became certain that Amelia had been telling the truth when she told them that she had seen Selina leave the house then return in a state of collapse when she was, so far as anyone knew, incapable of leaving her bed. Even Mrs Trevise, Selina's own mother, believed Amelia, but, besotted as he was, he had been convinced that, for some reason, they had all conspired to blacken Selina's name. Selina said she had not left the house and that it was the sudden sight of Amelia's face that had brought on the miscarriage. He should never have agreed to let Amelia stay in the house after Selina said she wanted her to go. It must have been a dreadful shock to suddenly see Amelia in her bedroom when she thought she was in Edinburgh with Grace. Yes, Selina must be telling the truth – she would never have had an abortion in spite of what the Doctor had said. How would she know where to find a Doctor willing to perform an illegal operation? He knew there were places prostitutes used when necessary but Selina was a respectable woman and would know nothing of such things. No, for some reason Amelia *had* told lies and he was better having no contact with her. His mind went back to his financial problems. There were several large bills he had put off settling until he had recouped. He realized that, unless he did something soon, he would be ruined and possibly in Debtor's prison. He would have to raise as much money as he could and he thought he knew the way.

Upon arriving at No.13 he found no fire laid in the dining room, only the cold ashes still in the grate from the previous day, nor had the table been laid for breakfast. He rang the bell vigorously until a flushed Jane, tousled-haired and dishevelled, made an appearance.

"Get this fire alight and inform your Mistress I wish to see her immediately," he ordered.

Jane opened her mouth, saw the set expression on his face and hurried to carry out his orders.

By the time Selina made a languid appearance the fire was well alight and John was striding impatiently up and down the room.

"Well? What do *you* want?"

"Sit down, Selina, I have some grave news."

Selina made a great fuss of selecting her chair and arranging her dress. She sat, playing with her pearl necklace. John stopped his pacing, leaned on the mantelpiece placing one foot on the fender.

"I'm in financial trouble. Why is irrelevant. We must retrench – drastically. I've decided that we will have to dispense with all but one servant..."

"*You* have decided to get rid of the servants! I hope you don't expect *me* to light fires and cook meals! If you are in trouble it is your own fault. Gambling I presume." She said, shrewdly.

He wondered how she knew but pushed that aside as unimportant – there were more pressing matters to consider.

"We will also have to sell the house and move to a smaller one – probably out in the suburbs. A small house would not be too difficult for you and a servant to manage. I may also have to sell your jewellery. That necklace for instance."

Selina sat very still. Then, slowly rising to her feet said, icily.

"These pearls were a present from a – friend. I will never consent to move from this house. You do not intend to remove me forcibly I presume?"

"Of course not but the house will have to be sold and you will have to leave whether you like it or not. If you stopped drinking perhaps we could start a family. It has been some years now, the Doctor could have been unduly pessimistic and I must have an heir."

"You must have an heir! I didn't marry you to provide you with an heir! Do you not understand. *I do not want children. I hate the very thought of children.* That's why I had the…"

She stopped and drew a sharp breath.

"You had what, Selina?" He asked, quietly.

"Nothing."

Taking hold of her shoulders he made her face him.

"Did you have an abortion, Selina?"

Selina knocked his hands away and shouted.

"Yes, I did and I'm glad – now are you satisfied?"

"So Amelia was telling the truth."

"I hated her from the beginning with her crooked face and her stupid designs. She should never have been born!"

"I believed you, Selina. I quarrelled with my mother and my sister on your account. Amelia could have been a great help to me in the business."

"The business, the business! What about *me*? I never go anywhere, I never see anybody.

"You could go out. You could go and see your mother. I'm sure she would love to see you."

"I told you, I never want to see my mother again. She said some dreadful things to me when she came to visit me after I lost the baby. She said I was selfish and self-centred. *ME!* She has been coming here trying to wheedle her way back in but I told Jane not to admit her. She came yesterday morning as a matter of fact. Now I'm going to bed – you've given me a headache."

"It's your drinking that has given you a headache, Selina."

Not bothering to reply she walked to the door. He called after her

"I'm going to go and see Amelia and ask her forgiveness. When I come back I shall expect to find you sober and able to have a rational conversation regarding our future."

Selina turned in the doorway.

"Don't you dare bring your ugly sister here! If she comes, I go."

When he did not reply she swept out of the room with a great rustling of skirts.

Following her into the hall he watched her walk unsteadily up the stairs.

As he drew a deep breath he noticed that the kitchen door was ajar. Moving swiftly he flung the door wide to find Mrs Merryweather and Jane standing at the top of the stairs leading down to the kitchen where they had been listening avidly.

"You can both take a week's notice."

Leaving them staring after him in shocked silence, he left the house and walked to Springfield Road. As he went he rehearsed what he would say.

Amy, resplendent in her hew housemaid's uniform, opened the door.

"Yes, Sir?"

"I wish to see Miss Wallace."

"What's yer name?"

"Mr Wallace. The matter is urgent."

"Wait 'ere."

As Amy shut the door Amelia came downstairs

"Was that someone at the door, Amy?"

"Yes, Miss."

"And who was it?"

"A Gent. Miss."

"And who did this 'Gent' want to see?"

"You, Miss."

"Did this gentleman have a name?"

'E said 'e was Mr Wallace, Miss."

Amy was startled to see Amelia go white and clutch the hallstand for support.

"You all right, Miss?"

"Yes. Where is Mr Wallace now? Has he gone?"

"Oh no, Miss I left 'im on the doorstep."

At this juncture the doorbell rang a sustained peal.

Amelia glanced in the hallstand mirror, straightened her blouse collar, drew a deep breath and ordered

"Open the door, Amy and show Mr Wallace into the dining room."

Mrs Trevise and Rose were at breakfast when Amelia entered and announced

"We have a surprise visitor."

As John entered the room behind Amy. Mrs Trevise looked up, puzzled.

"Who is..." seeing John she raised her hand to her mouth.

Rose, in the act of pouring a cup of tea, jumped and spilt the tea on to the tablecloth.

"Amy, fetch a cold cloth," she ordered sharply.

As Amy turned and ran towards the kitchen there was an awkward silence and John knew they were not going to make it easy for him.

Amy came back with a cloth and began to dab ineffectually at the brown tea stain spreading over the white cloth.

"Give that to me." Rose took the cloth out of her hand. "You may go."

"Yes, Mrs Brett. Thank you, Mrs Brett."

As she scrubbed the kitchen table Amy told Mrs Gipps

"There's somefink up. They ain't 'alf in a state. I knew this would be a bad day 'cos it's a Tuesday and they're always unlucky."

"Stop chattering girl, and peel those potatoes or you will be very unlucky!"

In the dining room Mrs Trevise broke the silence.

"Would you prefer us to leave you alone with Amelia, John?"

"No."

They waited. John considered how to begin. Then blurted out "Selena has just confessed to me that she lied, Amelia."

"At last!" breathed Mrs Trevise.

"Selina has decided to tell the truth at last and you have come here expecting me to welcome you with open arms!"

Amelia's face was flushed.

"Amelia has had a very bad chill, John. This is her first day out of bed. She insists on going in to her office although I have tried to persuade her not to. I am afraid that she is not herself."

Mrs Trevise soothed – in vain.

"I am most definitely myself, Aunt Isabella. I am not going to fall on his neck in floods of tears. This is not one of Rose's novels, this is real life and I don't feel like forgiving him."

Amelia folded her arms, defiantly.

Mrs Trevise rose from the table.

"I really do think it would be best if we left you both to talk things over. Come along, Rose."

Once they were alone John and Amelia faced each other. John was surprised to see that Amelia had turned into a young woman. For her part Amelia was shocked at how old John looked, his hair was going grey and his face was lined. But then, living with Selina was enough to age anybody, she reflected.

"Amelia, Mama has already forgiven me. I'll write and tell her that I have forgiven you. I'm sure she will be pleased."

"You have forgiven me! For what? Telling the truth?"

"I'm trying my best, Amelia. I am your brother and as such I have the right to expect..."

Amelia interrupted

"Does Selina know you are here?"

"Yes, I told her."

"And she will welcome me with open arms, I suppose?"

"To be honest, no, I don't think she will. She is not well but I'm sure that, once she recovers she will be pleased to see you."

He resolved to go straight home, remove all alcohol from the house and engage new servants with strict instructions not to supply Selina with any alcoholic drink on pain of instant dismissal without a reference.

"I should like to believe you, John, but I can't. Besides, I vowed when I left No 13 that I would never set foot inside while Selina was still there."

"That was many years ago, Amelia."

John was considerably put out. She was his youngest sister and should show him more respect.

"I would remind you, Amelia, that I am the head of the family and as such I can *order* you to leave here and come home with me."

"We had a similar conversation the last time you came here, John and my answer is just the same now as it was then. 'No'!"

John's face went a nasty shade of purple and thumping the sideboard in exasperation he shouted

"You are as stubborn as ever. How long are you going to keep this up, Amelia?"

"I have no intention of leaving Aunt Isabella. I am happy here. I'm glad that you know the truth at last and I'm sorry for you, John. You must have a miserable home life."

John felt very hard done by. He had come here willing to forgive Amelia only to have his forgiveness thrown back in his face by a stubborn and wilful young woman.

"That's enough. Your frankness will get you into trouble one of these days. I came here to affect a reconciliation but your attitude has made that impossible. When you come to your senses send me a message and I will come and fetch you home."

Amelia tossed her head. Not deigning to reply she rang the bell for Amy. Neither of them spoke. When Amy appeared Amelia ordered

"Show Mr Wallace out, Amy."

Then she turned her back and busied herself rearranging the ornaments on the mantelpiece.

John was extremely angry as he left the house. Really, Amelia had become worse than ever. That was the result of a houseful of women. They needed a man to keep them in order. It was a grave blow. He had fully expected that a relieved and grateful Amelia would be only too pleased to fall in with his wishes and return home after which her becoming his designer would naturally follow.

When Mrs Trevise and Rose heard Amy shut the front door they left the drawing room where they had taken refuge.

"Have you become reconciled?" Mrs Trevise asked, as she entered the dining room.

Amelia swung round from the mantelpiece and Mrs Trevise knew from her set and flushed face what the answer would be.

"No, Aunt Isabella, we have not and I don't think we ever shall."

"At least he knows now that you were telling the truth."

"He should have known before."

"You can't expect a man to believe his sister before his wife!"

"I don't want to discuss it any more. I must get ready or Bert will wonder where I am and I don't want to keep him waiting."

After Amelia had gone and they sat sipping the fresh tea that Rose had ordered, Mrs Trevise sighed and put down her cup.

"Oh dear, Rose. I don't think we have heard the last of this. I think I had better speak to Amelia tonight, perhaps she will feel better when she comes home."

"I've known Amelia all her life, Madam. She is probably already wishing she had not been so intractable but she can be very stubborn when she has made up her mind."

*****

All day John was pre-occupied with his financial worries. He decided not to announce any drastic measures to the workforce until he had explored every avenue. He worked late into the evening trying to find a way to rob Peter to pay Paul and arrived home, exhausted.

"Is Mrs Wallace in the drawing room?" He asked Jane as she took his coat.

"No, Sir, we haven't seen her all day. She left strict instructions that she was not to be disturbed. I went up to her room several times to ask her if she needed anything but she shouted at me to go away."

"And you haven't seen her at all today?"

"No, Sir. Perhaps she's ill. Madam is ill sometimes, Sir – if you know what I mean."

"That's enough. Go about your business."

Smirking, Jane disappeared through the kitchen door. So, even the servants had noticed Selina's drinking.

John ran upstairs to Selina's room. He found the curtains drawn and the gas lit but turned down low. He turned up the gas and saw that the room was in chaos. Clothes, shoes, stockings littered every surface. The dressing table was covered with empty jewellery cases, the contents piled in an untidy heap. He approached the bed where he could see Selina's form under the bedclothes.

"Wake up, Selina. We have to talk."

Getting no reply he shook her; there was no response. He shook her harder. Still no response. Looking round the room he noticed a glass on the washstand together with a small blue bottle. Picking up the bottle he read the label – laudanum. He turned back to the bed. She seemed very still. Pulling back the bedclothes he touched her shoulder. She was stone cold. With a shock he realized that she was dead. Had she killed herself or was it an accident? Either way there would be an inquest, publicity, scandal – a scandal he could ill afford. After thinking for a moment, he opened the heavy mahogany wardrobe, took down a hat box from the top shelf, placed the laudanum and glass at the back of the shelf, and replaced the hat box. He would retrieve them later when the servants were in bed. As he began to shut the wardrobe door he caught sight of himself in the mirror and was shocked to see how pale and drawn he had become. He slammed the door shut and, walking to the door called for Jane who appeared with uncharacteristic swiftness.

"Go and fetch Doctor Peters. Your mistress has been taken ill."

As he paced up and down the drawing room, waiting for the Doctor to appear, he ran over his actions and decided that there was nothing to raise the slightest suspicion of suicide.

When he heard Doctor Peter's voice he went out into the hall.

"It's Selina, Cedric. I don't seem able to wake her."

Doctor Peters nodded.

"Stay here, John. I know the way."

John waited at the foot of the stairs. After a brief interval Doctor Peters came down the stairs looking grave.

"Is Selina very ill?" John asked.

Doctor Peters did not answer him directly.

"You're going to need a stiff drink, John."

John followed him into the drawing room where the Doctor poured a generous measure.

"Sit down and drink up." He ordered.

John drank the whisky in one gulp.

"I'm afraid it's bad news. Selina is dead, John. I'm very sorry. It was her heart of course. It was never strong and the miscarriage weakened it still further."

"Will there be an inquest?"

"Oh no, perfectly straightforward. It was bound to happen sooner or later."

Taking a pad from his medical bag he sat down at the davenport, dipped a pen into the inkwell saying.

"I'll just write the Death Certificate then I must go."

"Did she suffer?"

"No, she would have known nothing about it. Is there anyone who can be with you?"

"I'll send for my mother and Selina's mother must be told."

"I'll leave you to it then."

As soon as Doctor Peters had departed John rang for Jane.

"Take a cab from the corner. Go to this address. Give this note to Mrs Trevise then bring her back with you. Here is the fare. Tell the cabby it is urgent."

While he waited for Mrs Trevise to arrive he went up to Selina's room. She lay in bed looking almost as she had when he married her. He sat and tried to work out what had gone wrong between them until Mrs Trevise, quietly entering the room, silently took her place on the other side of the bed.

CHAPTER THREE

Amelia was eager to talk things over with Arthur. She valued his commonsense approach and was disappointed when Higgins informed her that Mr Douglass had telephoned to say he would not be in until later in the day. She tried to work but found it very difficult to concentrate. She kept going over and over her encounter with John. She had to admit she had not handled it very well. She had allowed her tongue to run away with her – as usual! She didn't look forward to going home. Aunt Isabella and Rose were sure to insist on discussing the problem and all its implications. Realizing that she had been sitting staring at an uncompleted design for some considerable time she picked up a fine-nibbed pen and plunged it impatiently into the ink well. As she began to draw the pen spluttered ink over the paper. Snatching up a piece of blotting paper she began dabbing at the page but it was no good, the design was ruined, and she would have to begin again. Tearing the page from her sketch pad she screwed it up and flung it violently towards the waste paper basket which it missed. Sighing in exasperation, she got up from her desk, picked up the paper and put it into the waste basket. As she straightened she heard the door behind her open and, without looking round, said

"Get me some tea please, Miss Prentice. This is turning into a very bad day!"

Receiving no reply Amelia turned and was disconcerted to see not Miss Prentice, but a stranger. This was too much. She would never get anything done at this rate. Why couldn't salesmen make proper appointments!

"Yes, what is it?" she asked, ungraciously.

The visitor's gaze lingered on her face.

"Ah! I'm sorry. I expected to find Mr Douglass. I presume you are his Typewriter. Please inform Mr Douglass that I wish to see him."

"Mr Douglass is not available. I am Miss Wallace, Mr Douglass's Chief Designer as it states on the door. Can I help you?"

He blinked, disconcerted by her manner.

"A female designer – that is rather unusual is it not?"

Not waiting for a reply he brought out a card case, extracted a card and handed it to her.

Taking the proffered pasteboard she read

Rev. Edmund Milton

"My business is with Mr Douglass. Can you tell me when he will be available?"

"I believe he will be in later this afternoon."

Amelia replied, curtly.

"Thank you. Good afternoon."

Amelia escorted him to the door, opened it and called

"Miss Prentice!"

Miss Prentice looked up from her work.

"Would you show this gentleman out, please."

Bowing stiffly to Amelia he left the room. Feeling extremely disgruntled, Amelia went back to her design.

Soon afterwards Miss Prentice appeared with a welcome cup of tea.

"I thought you would like this, Miss Wallace."

Amelia took the cup gratefully.

"Thank you, Miss Prentice. I've had a trying day so far."

"I'll keep everyone away so that you don't get interrupted again."

"I can't think what Mr Higgins was about letting Mr. Milton just walk in like that."

"Mr Higgins is dealing with a serious problem in the factory. The gentleman just walked straight in. I thought he had an appointment with you."

"Well, it's not important. Thank you for the tea."

Taking the hint, Miss Prentice went back into Arthur's room shutting the door quietly behind her.

The rest of the day was peaceful and the new design went well. Amelia was feeling more cheerful when she got back home and was looking forward to a relaxing evening.

As soon as Amy opened the door she knew the last thing her evening would be was relaxed.

"OH! its awful, Miss!" Amy began excitedly.

"Broken some more eggs, Amy?" Amelia asked as Amy took her outdoor things and hung them on the hallstand.

"Oh no Miss. No, its Madam" she paused, dramatically.

Amelia's heart gave a jump.

"Aunt Isabella? What's happened girl? Is she ill? Have you sent for the Doctor?"

"Its not *our* Madam, Miss, it's the *other* Madam."

"Go slowly, Amy and begin at the beginning."

Taking her instructions literally Amy began at the point where, she, Amy got out of bed that morning. Eventually she arrived at the crux.

"A girl cum with a note for Madam. Madam takes the note and reads it then she goes like this" clutching at the bosom of her dress and rolling up her eyes "then I gets Mrs Brett, then Mrs Brett looks at the note and says 'Get Madam some brandy.' So I goes into the dinin' room and pours some brandy into a glass and takes it to Mrs Brett 'oo gives it to Madam 'oo…"

Amelia interrupted the flow

"Did Mrs Brett say what was the matter?"

"Yes, she did."

"Well, what was it?" Amelia had to stop herself from shaking the girl.

"Madam's daughter? The one wot she goes to see and she don't get let in? I think that's a crying shame Miss, 'er own daughter, I ask yer. I think…"

"WHAT HAS HAPPENED TO MADAM'S DAUGHTER?"

Amy looked aggrieved at being shouted at and said, with great dignity.

"She's dead and Madam's gone hoff in the cab to see 'er."

Amelia sat down hard on one of the hall chairs.

"Shall I get yer some brandy, Miss?" Amy asked, eagerly.

Amelia waved her hand.

"No, no. Where's Mrs Brett?"

"Upstairs I think and I said it were Tuesday!" Amy added, triumphantly.

Sometimes Amelia questioned the girl's sanity.

"I have no idea what you're talking about, Amy. No, please don't explain" as Amy opened her mouth "just go and ask Mrs Gipps to make me some tea would you."

As Amy scuttled off Amelia got up and walked into the drawing room. So, Selina was dead. Aunt Isabella must be very upset. A thought struck her and she rang the bell for Amy.

"Did Mrs Trevise say how Mrs John died?"

"No, Miss, she just said 'my poor Selina's dead' then she called for Mrs Brett, then I went back to the kitchen and told Mrs Gipps and she said…"

"Yes, thank you, Amy. That will be all."

"Yes, Miss. Thank you, Miss."

Amelia and Rose waited dinner until Mrs Gipps began to send messages from the kitchen that she could not keep it hot any longer.

As they ate Amelia asked.

"How do you think Selina died, Rose?"

"I have no idea. I expect Madam will tell us when she returns."

They continued their meal in silence. Just as they were about to rise from the table they heard the doorbell and a few minutes later Mrs Trevise came into the dining room. She looked old and tired. Going to her Amelia gently led her to a chair.

"Have you had anything to eat, Aunt Isabella? Rose can make you some soup."

"No, I don't want anything, thank you, Amelia. Selina is dead. Apparently it was her heart. We must think about mourning dresses. John has sent for his mother. I don't know when the funeral will take place. Next week I should imagine. There is such a lot to do. I must..."

"You must go to bed, Aunt and rest. Rose will bring you up some hot milk and you must promise me you will drink it."

"Perhaps I had better go to bed, I am rather tired. Thank you, Amelia. You are very good. Both of you. It has been such a shock."

"Come along, Madam, come with me." Rose led Mrs Trevise from the room.

Amelia wandered into the drawing room where she sat and thought of the day's events. John's unexpected arrival, Selina's death. At least Selina had lived long enough to confess to having the abortion. Ironic that, on the same day that she had told John she would not enter No.13 while Selina lived there, Selina had died. She knew she would be expected to go into mourning but what about the funeral? She did not want to go. She hadn't liked Selina when she was alive and she certainly didn't like her any better now she was dead. Perhaps she could say she was ill?

She put this suggestion to her Mother when she came the next evening to discuss the funeral arrangements with Mrs Trevise.

"Don't be ridiculous, Amelia. Of course you will attend. It is expected and John has enough problems. The servants left almost as soon as the Doctor had left the house. John asked them to stay until after the funeral but they refused and left the house there and then. I have had to hire temporary servants to help with the funeral feast. When I have time I shall engage more permanent staff, it is very inconvenient but then, as I told John you can't expect loyalty from servants."

"More tea, Madam" Rose enquired.

"No, thank you, Rose. As I was saying, Amelia, there is no question of you not attending the funeral."

"Yes, Mama" Amelia said, meekly.

"And you will not be going in to that office of yours until after the funeral it would not be seemly. In the meantime you can help Rose with sewing your mourning clothes."

"Yes, Mama."

Amelia had never mastered the art of dressmaking but thought it could not be that difficult. When she expressed this sentiment to Rose that lady rather tartly replied that

"Dressmaking is not something you can pick up in an afternoon, Amelia. Besides there is no need for you to do anything. Amy will help me. She tells me that she was taught plain sewing at the orphanage."

"I have to do something, Rose. Mama has forbidden me to go to the office."

"Very well. Here is some hemming. Make sure you keep the stitches even."

Amelia toiled diligently and by the end of the afternoon her fingers were sore from needle pricks, the material looked extremely limp, and even she had to admit that the stitches were anything but even.

"Do you think this will do, Rose?" She asked, doubtfully.

After inspecting her work Rose shook her head saying

"Why don't you go and design something Amelia?"

Amelia was only too pleased to comply and spent the rest of the week happily designing a musical box in the shape of a toy piano which was to look as if it was being played by a small mouse running over the keys.

Rose and Amy worked hard all the week and managed to complete the mourning dresses by the following Sunday when they all went to Morning Prayer as usual. It was the first time Amelia had been able to attend Church since the arrival of the new Vicar. She was considerably put out to find that the Celebrant was none other than the Rev. Edmund Milton. She knew she had been unnecessarily rude and wondered how he would react when he saw her. She spent the entire Service rehearsing what she would say to him but, when she went to speak to him, he ignored her and, addressing Mrs Trevise enquired

"I see you are in mourning, Mrs Trevise, not a close relative I trust?"

"My daughter, Mr Milton. My only daughter."

"I am very sorry to hear that. Shall we go and sit in the Church for a moment?"

They walked back into the Church passing a woman coming out who, seeing Rose and Amelia where they waited outside for Mrs Trevise, began making her way towards them.

"Amelia, that is the woman who found my brooch." Rose hastily informed her as the woman approached.

Amelia saw an elderly, high-coloured woman with startling green eyes. As soon as she came within speaking distance she asked

"You've had a family bereavement, Mrs Brett?"

Rose explained then said

"May I introduce you to Miss Wallace, Mrs Kitson."

Politenesses were exchanged after which Mrs Kitson asked

"Wallace – are you any relation to the Wallace's that own Wallace & Son? They make children's toys I believe?"

"Yes, I'm Mr John Wallace's sister."

"I see."

Mrs Kitson became very thoughtful then, aware that Amelia and Rose were looking at her expectantly she shook herself, smiled, and said

"I must get home. Good morning, Mrs Brett, Miss Wallace."

Rose gazed after her as she walked down the Church path to the gate.

"When Mrs Kitson smiled then I thought I knew her from somewhere. I wonder where it could have been?"

"You said she had just come down from Scotland. Perhaps you saw her when you came with me to Edinburgh to visit Grace and Gerald."

"Yes, of course, that must be it."

Soon after Mrs Trevise, dabbing her eyes with a black bordered handkerchief, came back to them saying

"The Vicar is a very kind, gentle person."

Amelia did not agree. She thought he was very rude not to acknowledge her presence just because she had been a little offhand. How was she to know he was not Miss Prentice? It was his fault for just walking in without waiting to be announced.

The day of Selina's funeral was fine. John had decreed that the funeral would be quiet with only the family present. Grace and Gerald could not attend due to the illness of their youngest child. There were very few flowers and only John, Sophia, Amelia and Mrs Trevise were present which Amelia thought was rather sad. After the short service and interment they returned to No.13. As the carriage stopped outside and she saw the familiar white marble pillars either side of the porch, the front door set back in its recess, the walls lined half-way up with blue and white tiles now sadly in need of cleaning, the black and white tiles on the floor almost unrecognisable under the mud and dirt, and the fanlight over the door filthy, the glass lozenge in the middle so dirty that the black 13 on it was almost indecipherable, she had a lump in her throat which had nothing to do with the funeral she had just attended.

Inside everything was as she remembered it, the wooden staircase leading upstairs, the iron hallstand. Only the pictures which used to cover the walls were missing leaving patches on the wallpaper. Beyond the staircase was the heavy mahogany door which she knew led to the kitchen. This was now propped ajar and a uniformed maidservant came up the kitchen stairs carrying a tray of food which she took into the dining room.

Amelia followed her mother, John and Mrs Trevise into the room where the table was laid with a cold collation.

The conversation was spasmodic and confined to general matters. Sophia said Grace and Gerald were sorry not to be present. They were extremely worried about their youngest boy who was running a high temperature. The Doctor strongly suspected measles. There was some discussion on the severity of the illness. Sophia said she hoped the Doctor was a good one as she had lost her infant son, George, to the same illness. The conversation lapsed and the meal was eaten in silence.

"If everyone has finished shall we go into the drawing room?" Sophia said.

Amelia sat by the window looking out into the garden. John took up his favourite position by the mantelpiece and Mrs Trevise and Sophia sat side by side on the sofa.

Nobody spoke until Mrs Trevise startled them all by saying

"Selina was very like her father you know. He would never acknowledge that he had made a mistake. No matter how much he might regret a decision he would never back down once he had made up his mind and it cost him his seat in Parliament. I am sure she wanted to see me but could not bring herself to admit it."

John remembered the last conversation he had had with his wife on the subject.

"Yes, I think she did. On that last day she as good as said she would like to heal the rift between you."

The look of pleasure tinged with sadness on Mrs Trevise's face made him glad he had told the lie. Selina was dead, and he saw no reason why she should continue to upset the living from beyond the grave. Pleased with the way he had handled the awkwardness he turned his attention to Amelia.

"Amelia, I have a proposition to put to you. I'm without a designer at the moment and I think it is time you came and worked for me."

No need to mention that he could no longer afford to pay a designer. He continued

"I know that it is something you have always wanted to do and you have proved your ability at Douglass's. The arrangement would suit me very well. Also" he was getting into his stride now "it would be more convenient if you came to live here with me."

She could not refuse in front of Mama he was sure. He desperately needed Amelia. She was an excellent designer and, more importantly, she would not cost as much as a male designer. He did not know how much Arthur was paying her but he knew it would not be even half the sum a good male designer could command. With a few cuts to the workforce and the money he had left from the sale of Selina's jewellery and the hall pictures, he was sure he would be able to weather the storm. He had another happy thought.

"In fact, Amelia, you can also run the household for me. You could do your designs here, at home. That way you can do both."

"I have already told you, John that I will not work for you." Amelia said, quietly.

"But it is your *duty* Amelia. I am the head of the family and I... I... *order* you to come back!" his voice rose.

Mrs Trevise said "Oh dear!" and put her hand to her mouth in horror.

Amelia went first red then white. She could not remember the last time she had felt so angry. But, before she could speak, Sophia intervened.

"I do not think this is an appropriate time for such a discussion, John. However, since you have raised the subject I must tell you that I have made up my mind to return here permanently. Grace can get on very well without me and as this was my home for many years I should like to live out my days here. Besides, Amelia, as she would be the first to admit, knows nothing about housekeeping. As for Amelia designing for you that is, of course, her decision."

They all looked at Amelia, waiting in their various ways for her reaction – John willing her to agree – Mrs Trevise afraid of what she might say – Sophia hoping she would make the right decision.

Amelia forced herself to speak quietly.

"I work for Arthur. I can't leave him especially at the moment. It is out of the question."

John was angry. If only Amelia had been born a boy there would be no difficulty as he would have automatically been taken into the business. Why had Amelia been given the gift of design and not himself? It would have made his life so much easier. He said, with as much dignity as he could command.

"I was hoping you had changed after all this time but you are as obstinate and awkward as you ever were."

"I think I will go into the garden." Amelia said, to no one in particular.

After she had left the room John sighed heavily.

"Go after her, John." Sophia urged.

"Do you think she will listen to me, Mother?"

"I don't know but you must try. She is your sister. If you don't heal the breach between you now it will never be healed which I am sure you will bitterly regret in years to come."

"Oh! Very well!"

From the window Mrs Trevise and Sophia watched John go out into the garden and speak to Amelia.

"I do hope they become friends again." Mrs Trevise said.

"As do I. I think more hangs on Amelia's decision than she realizes." Sophia replied.

In the garden John caught up with Amelia and walked by her side without speaking until they came to a garden bench. They both sat down and gazed intently at a recently dug over flower bed. Eventually John made an effort and said

"I really wish you would reconsider, Amelia. If not for me for the sake of the firm. I must have some designs for the Christmas trade or I shall have to put off most of the workforce. You may not realize it but unemployment is rife. I don't think they would be able to get work and their families could starve."

Amelia sat silently contemplating the neglected garden.

"Well, if you won't, you won't. You wouldn't know of course but, before you were born we lived in the middle of London. Papa began in a very small way and there were many problems and hardly any money. It was sometimes hard to make ends meet. Mama always wanted to move as she was convinced that it was the stale air of the City that killed our brothers and sisters. You saw how it still upsets her to speak of George. Both Papa and Mama worked hard building up the business and putting money by so that they could move into the new suburbs. Mama was so happy when they were able to move here and you were born. It could be the end of Wallace & Son, Amelia, and all our parents' hard work and sacrifice would be wasted. Papa would be so hurt if he knew that you refused to help."

"I'll design for you, John."

"You *will!*" he was overjoyed.

"But it must be on my terms."

"Anything – providing you don't want a large salary."

"I don't want a salary. I'll continue working for Arthur and design for you part time. Arthur must not know and I shall go on living with Aunt Isabella. She is getting old and needs me."

"I agree to everything. What made you change your mind?"

"It was something Rose said, many years ago. She told me how whole families could be plunged into poverty and misery when the wage earner lost his job through no fault of his own. I don't want that on my conscience."

John thanked God for Rose. He had always felt guilty about dismissing her. He remembered his father once telling him that they must always look after Rose. He suspected that Papa had known more about her past than any of them realized.

CHAPTER FOUR

Amelia felt guilty designing for John without Arthur's knowledge but she knew that Arthur, although a very fair man, was also a business man and would never countenance her working for what he considered to be a rival firm. Her father, William Wallace, had felt the same and, although the two families were quite close at one time, and frequently visited each other's houses, business was never discussed on these occasions.

She found designing in two different styles, although challenging, a great strain. She became very tired and never seemed to have time to sleep as she worked on John's designs into the early hours posting them to arrive the same day.

One evening in November, as they sat with their various occupations in the drawing room, Mrs Trevise put down her embroidery and asked

"Rose, do you think Amy is ready to wait on dinner guests yet?"

Rose considered

"Well, she has improved and hasn't dropped a plate for several weeks now."

"Sophia came to tea today and was telling me how disappointed she was not to be going to Edinburgh this Christmas. As Grace's youngest boy did not have measles after all Sophia had been looking forward to spoiling him. She had a letter from Grace this morning telling her that they have been invited to spend Christmas with Gerald's brother and his new wife. Of course she said she did not mind but I think she was very disappointed that she and John will be spending Christmas Day alone so I thought it would be nice to invite Sophia and John here for the day. Do you think that Amy could manage?"

"I've taught her how to deal with every situation that is likely to arise." Rose said.

"Good. I will send an invitation tomorrow and I'm going to insist that you sit down to Dinner with us as usual, Rose."

"I'm really not sure that would be acceptable." Rose demurred. "After all I was Mrs Wallace's housemaid for many years."

"That was a long time ago. You have moved on since then and I regard you almost as one of the family."

Rose shook her head, doubtfully.

"No, I won't hear any objections, Rose."

Mrs Trevise said, firmly.

"This is my house, not Mrs Wallace's, and I will run it as I think fit. I'm sorry if that offends you, Amelia."

"Not at all, Aunt. And I am sure Mama will not object. She may not approve but she would never be so rude as to mention it."

"Very well Madam, if that is what you wish." Rose said

"Besides" Amelia remarked "it will stop Rose following Amy and making her nervous. And you mustn't glare at her every time she makes a mistake, Rose."

"Do I glare at her?" Rose asked, shocked.

"Yes, you do. It must be very difficult for the poor thing. She is terrified of you!"

*****

It was Saturday afternoon and two days before Christmas. Amelia was on her own in the drawing room. Mrs Trevise was upstairs resting and Rose was out Christmas shopping. Amelia was taking the opportunity to wrap her Christmas presents. She decided to wrap Rose's first in case she came back early. She had bought her a complete morocco-bound set of novels by Charles Dickens. She couldn't wait to see her friend's face when she opened it. She had just completed wrapping the bulky parcel when she became aware of shouting, then a series of crashes. Were they being burgled? Quietly opening the door she slipped cautiously into the hall and listened. It sounded as if the noise was coming from the kitchen. She went swiftly along the hall to the kitchen door. She had no idea what she would do if confronted by a burglar. Taking a deep breath she entered the room to find the kitchen floor covered in broken china and two figures struggling on the tiled floor while Mrs Gipps hit them indiscriminately with the carpet beater as she shouted.

"Stop it! Stop it, you little devils!"

Walking further into the room Amelia could see that one of the combatants was Amy who was sitting on the chest of a young man while she punched his head. He was defending himself as best he could and shouting at the top of his lungs.

Going to the sink Amelia filled a jug with cold water and threw it over them both. As they gasped Mrs Gipps threw down the carpet beater and, grabbing Amy and the youth by the backs of their collars, pulled them both upright, one in each hand.

Amy stood with her head bowed, dripping water, her cap a soggy mess, her hair in rat's tails while the youth struggled and spluttered.

"Wotcher 'anging on to me for? I 'ant done nofink! She started it. I only said..." Then, seeing Amelia he stopped.

"You only said?"

"Nofink, Miss."

"Mrs Gipps, do you know what provoked Amy into attacking him?"

"Yes, Miss but I am not going to repeat it."

"Make 'er let go of me, Miss. I could 'ave the law on yer!"

Mrs Gipps shook the boy.

"You little devil! I'll tell your master and you'll lose your place."

He wriggled harder.

"Look at 'er! She *is* ugly!"

Mrs Gipps let go of Amy in order to cuff him round the ear.

Amelia sighed.

"Don't hit him, Mrs Gipps, he was only telling the truth."

The boy blushed.

"Sorry, Miss." He mumbled.

"I'll tell his Master, Miss. He deserves to lose his place. It's not for him to make remarks about his betters."

"Let me have him, Mrs Gipps. Amy, stay here. I'll speak to you in a moment. What is your name, young man?"

"Ned, Miss. I'm the Butcher's boy."

"Well come along, Ned."

Ned picked up his cap from the floor, wrung it out, placed it firmly on his head and followed Amelia into the hall where, regaining his dignity he said

"I'll get a Policeman to 'er. She's mad!"

"No, you won't and I won't complain to your Master. We'll forget it ever happened. Here, take this and buy something to soothe your bruises."

Opening the hallstand drawer she felt round for the lose change which she knew was always kept there for emergencies and, bringing out a handful of coins, handed them to the boy. As Ned counted them his eyes widened.

"Cor! Thank you, Miss. And you ain't that ugly!"

Amelia laughed as she opened the front door and pushed him through.

"Well, thank you, Ned. Now off you go or you *will* lose your place."

Back in the kitchen she found Amy crying bitterly.

"She's afraid she'll be turned off and I wouldn't blame you if you did, but she is a willing girl and I'm sure she'll never do anything like it again. And the crockery can come out of her wages."

Mrs Gipps handed Amy a handkerchief. Amy blew her nose and wiped her eyes then, screwing the handkerchief into a wet ball, pleaded

"Please don't send me away, Miss. I like it 'ere and I ain't got nowhere else to go. I don't want to go back to 'er. Please don't tell Mrs Brett or she'll send me away for sure."

"I've no intention of telling Mrs Brett, Amy. But please remember in future that I can fight my own battles. I've had long enough to learn." She added, bitterly.

"Oh, thank you, Miss. I'll work 'ard, I promise."

They all turned as Rose came in through the back door and gazed in horror at the chaos.

"Amy! What have you done?"

Mrs Gipps spoke before Amy could reply.

"I'm very sorry, Mrs Brett. Amy was carrying in the dirty breakfast things when she tripped over the cat and dropped the tray."

"Cat? We don't have a cat, Mrs Gipps."

"Next door's cat must have got in and... and hidden somewhere and darted out just as Amy was coming into the kitchen." Amelia said.

"That's right." Mrs Gipps said "dratted thing!"

"Where is the cat now?"

Amelia and Mrs Gipps spoke together.

"We pushed it out into the garden." Amelia said.

"It ran away somewhere." Mrs Gipps said.

"Why are you dripping wet, Amy?"

Amelia and Mrs Gipps exchanged anguished looks.

"Well, Mrs Brett, it's 'cos of the cat."

"Can you explain to me why you falling over a cat should make you wet?"

Rose patiently enquired.

"Well, it was a black cat and they're unlucky so, if yer fall over one yer must cover yerself with water to stop the evil gettin' at yer."

Amelia thanked Heaven for Amy's obsession with superstition although she had a shrewd idea that this myth, like most of the others, was probably a figment of Amy's imagination.

"I see." Rose said, thoughtfully. "Are you badly hurt? Come here, let me see."

Amy reluctantly went to Rose who inspected her face.

"It looks worse than it is. We will put something on your eye. I'm afraid you will not look very pretty for a while. Show me your hands."

Reluctantly Amy held out her hands for inspection, the knuckles were badly grazed.

"Hmm. We must put some ointment on these. Perhaps you would do that, Mrs Gipps."

"Certainly, Mrs Brett."

"I expect Amy grazed her hands trying to stop falling over don't you, Miss Wallace?"

"I should imagine so, Mrs Brett. Amy has offered to pay for the damage out of her wages."

"I don't think that's necessary. It was an accident after all. Did you come in here for something?"

"I heard the crash and came to see what had happened. I think I'll go back to the drawing room. Please don't come in. I'm busy at the moment."

"Very well. I'll stay and help Mrs Gipps clear up the mess. You must go and change out of those wet clothes, Amy, then you can come back and help."

Amy fled.

Amelia had a suspicion that Rose had not believed the story of the cat but, with her usual good sense, had decided not to enquire further. She wished she could be like Rose and think first before she spoke. Her impulsiveness was always getting her into trouble.

After a few days the incident was forgotten in the bustle of Christmas preparations.

At the Works, Amelia, Miss Prentice and Mr. Higgins worked hard addressing individual envelopes for the whole workforce. Arthur liked to write personal Christmas cards thanking each man by name for all his efforts during the year and enclosing an extra week's wages.

At Springfield Road Mrs Gipps was instructed to make extra plum puddings and mince pies. Amy and Rose spent hours cleaning the house from top to bottom.

A small fir tree was purchased and placed in the drawing room window. Amelia volunteered to decorate it with small presents and bunches of sweetmeats, finishing the whole thing off with tiny wax candles.

Eventually all the Christmas Cards were written and posted, the food prepared, the decorations up and the house cleaned until it shone.

According to their usual custom, on the afternoon of Christmas Eve presents were exchanged.The servants receiving theirs first.Amy was overcome to receive a cookery book from Rose, a muff from Amelia and a bolt of silk for a new walking-out dress from Mrs Trevise.

"Oh! Thank you! I ain't never had no presents before!"

She told them, excitedly.

Mrs Trevise handed Mrs Gipps an envelope.

"Thank you, Madam. Come along, Amy."

Without opening it Mrs Gipps tucked the envelope into her apron pocket and ushered out an excited Amy clutching her presents.

"Do you think she was telling the truth when she said she had never had any presents?" Amelia asked, shocked.

"I'm afraid so." Rose replied.

"Now it's our turn for presents."

Mrs Trevise reminded them. Amy and her sad past were forgotten as they unwrapped presents, and exclaimed over each one.

Christmas Day was very cold but dry. John and Sophia entered the drawing room to find the three ladies sipping sherry. Rose rather nervously awaited Sophia's reaction to her presence. Seeing this Mrs Trevise rose to her feet saying

"It is so nice to see you both. I have given the servants the afternoon off once dinner has been served. Amy is spending the rest of today and tonight with Mrs Gipps who has kindly invited her to spend Christmas with her and her large family. I'm sure Amy would much prefer that to sitting on her own in the kitchen. As the only living-in servant it must be lonely at times."

Saying nothing Sophia nodded her head in agreement.

"Pour Sophia and John a sherry would you, Rose dear?" Mrs Trevise continued.

Rose, feeling extremely awkward, complied. John took his sherry with a smile of thanks, Sophia indicated a small table by her armchair. Mrs Trevise and John began an animated conversation on the design of gardens. As Rose placed the glass of sherry on the table Sophia said, in a low voice.

"I am so pleased to see how you have risen in life, Rose. I am sure you are a sensible woman and will not take advantage of Mrs Trevise's kindness. Not many servants enjoy your privileges you know."

Rose flushed and bit her lip.

"I have no intention of taking advantage of anyone, Mrs Wallace. All I want to do is to stay with Amelia until she no longer needs me."

"That sentiment does you great credit, Rose."

Rose was relieved when the conversation was interrupted by Amy, who entered the room, resplendent in a new apron and cap, cleared her throat and, remembering Rose's instructions to speak clearly, announced in ringing tones

"DINNER HIS SERVED!"

To Rose's great relief there were no major incidents during dinner. Mrs Gipps had excelled herself. Amy vindicated all Rose's hard work and did not drop a single plate. There was one awkward moment when Sophia saw Amy's black eye. When Rose explained that Amy had tripped over the cat, John asked, surprised.

"Do you have a cat? I haven't seen it. What is it called? I rather like cats."

"It was next door's cat which now seems to have vanished. Probably didn't like being trodden on." Rose explained. She almost said 'Sir' but managed to stop herself in time.

After they had repaired to the drawing room the conversation naturally turned to the events of the dying year.

"Thank you for all your work, Amelia." John said "I think I can say that you helped save the firm."

It was on the tip of Amelia's tongue to protest that she had been pushed into doing the designs instead she said

"I am glad I could help."

"I'm sure Amelia was only too pleased to help you, John." Sophia said. "Although I have never understood how the firm got into such a state."

"It was a matter of business, Mother. Nothing for you to worry about. We are out of the woods now."

Or they would be if he did well at the tables which he must as it was a New Year and things were bound to improve.

"I wonder what 1886 has in store for us." Mrs Trevise said, rather apprehensively.

Seeing that Mrs Trevise was becoming melancholy Amelia hastened to reassure her.

"Nothing but good things, Aunt, I'm sure."

Rose got to her feet.

"If you will excuse me, I have to speak to Amy."

After she had left the room Sophia said

"I remember when Rose's mother came to me and asked me to take Rose on as a servant. It was the day you were born, Amelia. I must admit that she has been a good servant to you."

"She is not my *servant*, Mama, she is my *friend*."

"Well, we won't argue today of all days. I think it is time we went home, John, it is getting late."

They all rose and goodbyes were said.

After she had seen them out Amelia went back into the drawing room and stood gazing into the fire.

"What is the matter, Amelia. Do you feel unwell?" Mrs Trevise asked, anxiously.

"I feel perfectly well. It's just that I wish Mama would understand that Rose is my friend."

"It is difficult for her. You must remember that Rose was her servant for many years and we do have a very unconventional household."

"I hope that Rose will always stay here with me."

"Of course she will. She is too old to think of marriage and you are hardly likely to – oh I didn't mean to say that, Amelia. It must be the wine, I'm so sorry."

"But you are quite right, Aunt – who would want to marry an ugly looking thing like me!"

"It's not like you to be self-pitying, Amelia."

"No. Rose would be extremely annoyed with me, but it's hard Aunt. I walk down the street and people stare – they always have. I never used to mind but just lately… "

"Lately you've come to realize what you will be missing – a husband, children, a home of your own. It is very unfair but you must learn to accept it."

"I know. I think I will ask Mr Milton how I can become a Nun!"

"And give up designing? Obey orders without question? I don't think you would like that. Besides what would I do without you?"

"I'm sorry Aunt, of course I'll stay with you. It is just that sometimes I feel so… so *different*."

"I expect you are tired, my dear. It has been a long and tiring day but very enjoyable and now I am going to bed. Don't stay up too long brooding will you?"

"No Aunt – good night."

Once she was alone Amelia did something she had not done for a long time. She went to the overmantel mirror and studied her face. Normally she avoided mirrors unless it was absolutely necessary. Now she looked hard at herself. The right side of her face was normal but the left side looked crooked as if somebody had pulled it down. She tried smiling at herself. The smile was crooked. Why did she have to be different? Soon she would be twenty-six and well and truly 'on the shelf'. She knew that nobody would want to marry her but it would have been nice to have a family like other women. It was all very well for Rose to tell her it was what was on the inside that mattered not the outside but it was the outside that everyone saw, not the inside, as Ned's remarks proved. She didn't know which was worse, people remarking on her appearance or going out of their way to ignore it. Resolutely turning from the mirror she told herself that this self-pitying must stop and went to bed where it took her a long time to go to sleep which had nothing to do with the room being freezing cold.

The weather after Christmas was severe. The thick frost lasted all day. In spite of wearing mittens and sitting close to the blazing office fire, Amelia was cold all the time. She was grateful for Bert's arm as he escorted her from the office building and across the icy pavement to the cab which, in spite of the straw strewn liberally on its floor, was freezing cold. As he left her at her door he admonished her

"You be careful, Miss. Wait for me to come and give you an 'and termorrer."

"I will Bert, thank you."

Amy opened the door to her ring.

"Come in quick, Miss. Let me take yer cloak and bonnet."

"Thank you, Amy."

"Madam and Mrs Brett are in the drawin' room, Miss. I was just gettin' a nice cup of tea."

Amelia found Mrs Trevise writing letters and Rose mending a patchwork quilt.

"I recognize that quilt, Rose. It's the one you brought with you when you came, isn't it? I remember you showing me the piece of material Mama gave you. Which one is it? I can't remember."

"It's this one."

Rose pointed out a square of material covered with tiny biege flowers on a blue background.

"Oh yes, I remember now. That was from one of Mama's dresses wasn't it?"

"Yes, it was. It's very faded now."

Amy knocked and entered.

"Mrs Kitson to see you, Madam." she said in her best parlourmaid voice.

Mrs Trevise rose as Mrs Kitson entered the room.

"You must be frozen! Do come and sit by the fire."

Mrs Kitson did not appear to hear. She was gazing fixedly at the quilt which Rose was still holding.

Mrs Trevise was concerned.

"Are you unwell, Mrs Kitson? Amelia, fetch Mrs Kitson some brandy."

"No, no brandy. I'll be fine in a moment, just let me sit down."

She sank down into an armchair by the fire.

"You should not be out in this cold weather. You look very pale. Are you sure there is nothing I can get you?"

"I am quite well, thank you, Mrs Trevise."

Amy came in bearing the tea tray which she placed on the small table by the fire saying

"Please Madam, Mrs Gipps says would it be all right if she goes 'ome early. She's worried about the little 'uns falling' in the fire as 'annah – 'er eldest – is in bed with a cold."

"Tell Mrs Gipps that she may go home as soon as she wishes. And Amy"

"Yes, Madam."

"Tell her to take Hannah some of that broth will you? That will be all, thank you."

"Yes, Madam. Thank you, Madam."

Mrs Trevise began pouring tea into cups.

"Do have some, Mrs Kitson. It will warm you up and also some of this fruit cake. Mrs Gipps only baked it this morning."

"Thank you. No cake, thank you. That is a very nice quilt, Mrs Brett. Did you make it yourself?"

"Yes, when I was very young. I was just showing Miss Wallace one of the squares from her mother's dress."

Mrs Kitson made several attempts before she asked

"You have known Miss Wallace a long time?"

"Oh yes, I went to work for Mrs Wallace the day Amelia was born."

They were alarmed when Mrs Kitson fell back into her chair with a moan, dropping her cup and saucer with a crash onto the hearth where they shattered.

"Fetch me my smelling salts, Amelia. They are on my dressing table." Mrs Trevise ordered.

Amelia flew upstairs and got the smelling salts which Mrs Trevise took from her and waved under Mrs Kitson's nose. They waited anxiously and were relieved when she coughed and opened her eyes.

"Are you better now?" Amelia asked, anxiously.

"Yes, much better. Mrs Trevise, Miss Wallace I have to ask a great favour. Could I please speak privately to Mrs Brett? It is very important."

"Of course, come Amelia, we will go into the dining room."

Greatly puzzled Amelia followed Mrs Trevise into the dining room where she lit the fire ready laid in the grate. It was very cold.

Mrs Trevise shivered.

"Let me fetch you a shawl, Aunt."

"Thank you, Amelia. It is rather chilly."

As Amelia placed the pink woollen shawl round Mrs Trevise's shoulders she asked

"Why do you think Mrs Kitson wanted to see Rose alone?"

"I have no idea. It is not our business. Rose will tell us if she thinks we need to know."

Amelia would have liked to discuss the matter but knew her Aunt's strong aversion to gossip.

They sat, staring into the fire for some time. When they heard Amy close the front door they exchanged a glance.

Immediately Rose came into the room it was clear that she had been crying. Amelia went to her in concern.

"Whatever is the matter, Rose?"

With uncharacteristic vehemence Mrs Trevise said

"If Mrs Kitson has said anything to upset you, Rose I'll forbid her the house!"

"No, no you must not – she is my mother!" Rose began to cry.

"Your mother? But I thought she was dead!"

"So did I, Amelia. The last I heard of her was a letter from the Housekeeper where she was employed. We had run away from my stepfather. Your Mama very kindly gave me a position as a housemaid. My Mother wrote to me several times but when the letters stopped I wrote to the Housekeeper. She wrote back telling me that my stepfather went to the house and made a scene and as a result my mother was dismissed."

"How awful. He was a horrible man, Rose."

"He was, Amelia and very cruel. I waited for Mother to write as she said she would but no letter came so, in the end, I went to Ratcliff Court to find her but only found my stepfather. He tried to make me stay with him and, when I said I wouldn't, he tried to drag me inside the house. I had to hit him to get away. All he would tell me was that she had run away. I didn't know whether to believe him or not. Your Papa was very good to me, Amelia. He asked his friend in the Police to try and find her. The Inspector did his best but there was no sign of her. When my stepfather got arrested for stealing your Papa's designs and sent to prison, I expected Mother to come but she never did. In the end I decided that she was dead."

"If your stepfather was in prison there was nothing to stop your mother finding you. Are you certain she is your mother?"

Amelia queried.

"There is no doubt. She knows all about my father and how he got killed. What a struggle we had to survive. How she had to take in lodgers – everything. She described how she hit my stepfather with a poker and crippled his arm. Nobody else knew that except your Papa and she remembered how she had given me her brooch the day your Mama employed me as a housemaid. Only my mother could possibly know that."

"But why didn't she get in touch with you?" Amelia persisted.

"She didn't know that my stepfather was in prison. She was afraid he would find her again. She didn't want to lead him to me. She changed her name and took various jobs, ending up as Housekeeper to a wealthy mill owner in Edinburgh. When he died he left her a large sum of money which she invested and, as a result, she is now quite wealthy."

Amelia and Mrs Trevise were enthralled.

"Go on." Amelia urged as Rose paused for breath.

"She lived in a house just outside Edinburgh for many years but she never forgot me and, in the end, she had to come and find me. She decided to begin her search on the Monday after her arrival. On the Sunday she went to St. Mary's for Morning Prayer. When she picked up my brooch she could not believe it. She had to see who had dropped it. She was almost sure when she saw me and the feeling that she was right has been getting stronger each time we met. She spent Christmas alone in her hotel room thinking it over and today she could not stand the uncertainty any longer so she came here to find out the truth – how she had no idea but, as soon as she saw my quilt she knew."

Rose stopped, exhausted.

"I'm so glad, my dear." Mrs Trevise went to Rose and hugged her.

"So am I, Rose. But, does your mother know about your stepfather – what he did?"

"Yes, I told her everything.

"Was she very distressed?" Mrs Trevise asked.

"Yes. She asked me if I knew where he was now. I told her what the Police told us that he had probably escaped to the Continent and that if he came back he would immediately be arrested for murder so there was nothing to worry about. I did my best to get her to stay for a while to recover but she insisted on going back to her hotel. She refused to let me go with her."

"She is probably better on her own."

"Do you know the name of her hotel?" Amelia asked.

"Yes. I thought, if you don't need me, Madam, I would go to see her tomorrow. She is talking of buying a house that we can share."

Mrs Trevise glanced at Amelia. She knew this would be unwelcome news. She asked the question that she knew Amelia lacked the courage to ask.

"What have you decided to do, Rose?"

"I don't know. I promised not to leave Amelia but then Mrs Kitson is my mother. I don't know what to do."

Rose began to cry afresh.

"Do what you think is best, Rose." Amelia urged her.

"I'll be sorry to see you go." Mrs Trevise said "although it might not be for some time – Mrs Kitson has to find a house first."

"Yes, of course. There is no need to make a decision just yet." Rose agreed, wiping her eyes.

CHAPTER FIVE

Although it was bitter January weather and dark, Amelia was relieved to get back to work even if the office was cold.

Arthur spent more and more time at home with Eleanor. One Monday morning, towards the end of January, Amelia's telephone jangled. Upon answering it she heard Arthur's voice.

"Hello, Arthur. Is anything wrong?"

"It's Eleanor. We have had a dreadful time with her. We have been up all night. She refuses to go to bed and walks round and round the house all night checking the doors and windows. We are both exhausted and the servants have given notice."

"Oh dear, have you sent for the Doctor?"

"Yes, he has just left. That's why I'm telephoning. I'm sorry to put this burden on you, Amelia, but the Doctor insists that Eleanor be removed from London and all its associations. He says he thinks she is suicidal. He wants her to go to a special Clinic in Bournemouth that has some new treatment called Mesmerism and we have agreed. Naturally, Patience is very upset and wants to be near her so we are going to rent a house near the Clinic. We're catching the 3.15 train. Do you think you can manage if I leave you and Mr Higgins in charge? You don't need to worry about dealing with the Works, Mr. Higgins can do that, but if you will keep an eye on things in the office for me it would be a great help. I'm sorry it's such short notice."

"I'm sure we can manage, Arthur. How long do you think you will be away?"

"I've no idea. Of course I will be come up to town regularly to deal with anything urgent. If you can manage with Mr. Higgins' help it would be a weight off my mind."

"We will manage perfectly, Arthur. I hope Mrs Jarrett will soon recover."

"I'll telegraph you my address as soon as I can and you telegraph me if there is anything urgent."

"Of course, Arthur, don't worry."

"Thank you, Amelia. I knew I could rely on you. I have already spoken to Mr. Higgins and he is quite happy with the arrangement."

After going over various urgent business matters he rang off.

Amelia felt elated and a little anxious. How many women in London were thought capable of being left in charge of a business enterprise? Now was her chance to prove she was just as capable as any man.

For the next few weeks Amelia worked hard familiarizing herself with the running of the office. She spent her mornings dealing with the post and dictating replies to Miss Prentice, and her afternoons designing. When she got home she spent her evenings and late into the night working on designs for John.

As she was responsible for the running of the firm she had expected Mr Higgins to give her regular reports. She was considerably annoyed therefore when, in answer to all her enquiries regarding the Works he smiled and said

"Everything is proceeding as Mr Douglass would wish, Miss Wallace."

She reluctantly accepted this until she learnt from Miss Prentice that there had been some trouble in the Works and decided to confront the Chief Clerk without delay. Arthur had left her in charge with Mr. Higgins as her assistant and Arthur would, therefore, hold her responsible for any problems which arose in his absence.

"Ask Mr. Higgins to come to my office, Miss Prentice."

She waited in some impatience but it was some hours later that Mr Higgins finally entered her office by which time she was extremely annoyed.

"You wanted to see me, Miss Wallace?"

"Yes, Mr. Higgins. Miss Prentice tells me there is some sort of problem in the Works."

"Nothing I can't deal with. Just leave it to me."

"Mr Douglass asked me to keep an eye on things and I can hardly do that if I am not kept informed, can I?"

"It is a Works matter. Nothing for you to worry about. I know these men – I can deal with them."

"Well at least tell me what the problem is."

Amelia insisted.

Mr. Higgins sighed – he wished Mr Douglass would come back. Dealing with forceful females at work as well as at home was not his idea of a peaceful life. He couldn't imagine what Mr Douglass thought he was about giving Miss Wallace the impression that she was in charge when it was obvious that Mr Douglass had intended that he should have the responsibility.

"It's some idea the men have in their heads that they want to start one of these Unions. Its just a whim, it'll soon pass."

"A Union. Is that so terrible?"

"The Social Democratic Federation are holding a big rally today in Trafalgar Square. The men in the Works have elected a spokesman who has informed me that he has decided to go to the meeting and represent the men in support of their 'brothers'. I told Jarvis, the spokesman, that he was perfectly at liberty to go so long as he realized he would not be paid for the time he took off. I think you will find he will change his mind once he realizes he is going to lose a day's wages. Most employers would have sacked him on the spot."

Mr. Higgins said, confidently.

"I should like to speak to this Jarvis and find out what all this is about."

"I don't think that is a good idea, Miss Wallace. I have dealt with the matter and I think you will find there is nothing to worry about. Also you are a woman and the men have very fixed ideas about the role of men and women."

"Have they. Well thank you for the information, Mr Higgins."

Amelia said, frostily.

"I'm sorry, Miss Wallace, but that is how things are. There is nothing I can do about it."

Amelia had to concede that, if Mr. Higgins had dealt with the matter, it would be unproductive to stir it all up again.

"Very well, Mr Higgins. That will be all."

Amelia sat thinking for a while. Making up her mind she got up, took her cloak and bonnet from the coatstand and went into Arthur's room.

"Miss Prentice, I am going out. I will be back later. If Mr. Higgins asks where I am tell him that I have gone out on business."

She wanted to find out what this Union business was all about. Years ago she had attended meetings of the National Union of Women's Suffrage and assumed it was a similar organization. She felt that somebody from the firm should investigate and Mr. Higgins was obviously not going to do it so she would have to.

Once outside the building she hailed a cab and instructed the cabby to take her to Trafalgar Square.

"Are you sure, Madam? There's a big rally going on. Why don't you just go home instead?"

"Trafalgar Square please, cabby." Amelia said, firmly.

"Well, don't say I didn't warn you."

As they made their way along Piccadilly the crowds got thicker and the cab had a job making any progress. In the end it stopped, caught in a jam of pedestrians and other horse-drawn traffic.

"Can't go any further. You'll have to walk from here."

Amelia paid the cabby and descended into the street. The whole road was full of men all going in one direction. She didn't see any other women but there must be some somewhere. She was sure the NUWS would support the men.

As they got nearer to Trafalgar Square the crowd became even denser and she could hardly move.

At first she was totally ignored but, as they got closer to the Square, she saw glances cast in her direction. Her face again, she thought.

She had just begun to wonder whether this was such a good idea when the crowd behind her suddenly surged forward and she grabbed at the man in front to prevent herself from falling over.

The man turned round. Seeing Amelia he looked first surprised and then annoyed.

"Go home, woman. This is man's work."

"But I'm interested. I want to hear the speaker. I used to go to the NUWS meetings."

Several men looked in her direction, attracted by the sound of a woman's voice.

"The Women's Suffrage is just a load of women with time on their hands. Get back to where you belong – at home with your children."

The man impatiently replied.

"I don't have any children."

"I'm not surprised with a face like that!" Another man joined in. "Enough to curdle the milk that face is!"

"There's no need to be rude!" Amelia hotly retorted.

"What are you doing here anyway? Are you unemployed?"

The first man enquired.

"No, I'm not."

"What are you then? A factory girl?"

"Not dressed like that she 'aint!"

From a man behind her.

More and more heads were beginning to turn in her direction.

"I'm a toy designer."

"Are you. See all these men? They're unemployed and I'll tell you why, because women are taking their jobs. And why are the employers taking them on? Because they work for half the wages of men."

"If women were paid the same as men they could compete with men on an equal footing." Amelia argued.

"Everyone knows women are only good for one thing." A large man sneered.

Amelia raised her voice trying to get above the laughter that this sally raised.

"That's no answer! Women should have the same rights as men. We are all people after all – "

"But God made Adam first, woman. That's why men have more rights than women." The man told her, triumphantly.

Several other voices agreed.

Amelia's temper, always ready to ignite, flared.

"That's a stupid thing to say!"

"Who are you calling stupid?"

"You are stupid if you can't see that it's in everyone's interest for women to be treated equally with men!" She declared.

There was an angry murmur and it was at this point Amelia realized she could be in a very dangerous position. There was no way she could get out of the crush and the men were becoming angry. She tossed her head, defiantly – she was not going to give in to these idiots.

She jumped when her arm was firmly grasped from behind and a voice spoke in her ear.

"You shouldn't be here, Miss Wallace. Come with me."

Turning round with difficulty she was amazed to see Mr Milton.

"That's right – take her home where she belongs!"

"You should keep your wife under control!"

Amelia was extremely angry. How dare Mr Milton tell her what to do!

"But I don't want…"

"Things are turning very ugly. The Police are on their way. You're coming with me."

"No, I'm…"

She was dragged, protesting loudly, through the crowd. Mr Milton seemed to be very strong and very determined. Holding her arm firmly he barged his way forcefully through the crowd to the obvious delight of the men who gave him advice on what to do with her when he got her home some of which Amelia did not understand. He pushed her through a doorway. She saw tables and waitresses in neat uniforms and realized that he had taken her to Lyons Corner House. Mr Milton did not release her until he had seated her at a secluded table for two. A waitress instantly materialized – pencil poised over pad.

"A pot of tea for two and a selection of cakes, please." He calmly ordered.

"Certainly, Sir."

The waitress gave no hint that it was in any way unusual for a gentleman to drag a lady into the establishment.

"I think you should visit the Ladies Room, Miss Wallace. You are looking rather dishevelled and you have several smuts on your nose."

Amelia was in two minds whether to get up and walk out but she could feel her back hair coming down and her bonnet seemed to be half on and half off. Burning with rage, she rose in as dignified a manner as she could manage and asked the waitress for directions to the Ladies Room, where the attendant tutted and offered her assistance which Amelia declined. Looking in the mirror she was startled to see that she looked a wreck. Her hair had given up the struggle and hung half-way down her back, her bonnet had not only lost its black ostrich feather but was badly crushed and, she peered into the mirror, she did have several nasty black smuts on her nose. As she repaired the damage, she debated whether to walk straight past him and go home. But she was hungry, not having had any lunch. A cup of tea and a cake would not do any harm and he had rescued her – she supposed. She would take tea with him but she would be very distant.

When she returned to the table Mr Milton said approvingly

"That's much better. You look more like yourself. However did you manage to get caught up in the riots?"

"I didn't get 'caught up'. I went to hear the speaker."

"Why on earth did you want to do that? It's…"

"Yes, I know," she interrupted, wearily, "men's business. Well I think it is about time women had a say in things."

She bit viciously into a chocolate cream cake.

"I was going to say that it is unusual to find a woman who understands what it is all about, let alone joins in."

"Oh, I know what it is about. It is about rights. Women should have the same rights as men. I have heard Ann Wilton speak."

Amelia said, triumphantly as she selected another cake.

"So have I and I agree that women should be allowed to vote and take their place in Society."

Amelia choked on a piece of Dundee.

"You do!"

"Yes, but you can't do it all on your own. These men want decent hours of work and better working conditions. Some of the conditions they work in are appalling. I spend a great deal of my spare time at St. George's in the East helping my friend who is the incumbent. He is trying to start a Mission to help these people. You can't blame them for not being interested in what they see as a frivolous concern which could take attention away from their problems. Once they have achieved their demands, if they ever do, they might be more inclined to listen. I don't think you really understood what it was all about, did you?"

"No, perhaps not." Amelia conceded.

"And you must admit that going to the Square on your own was a very foolish thing to do, Amelia."

Neither of them noticed his use of her Christian name.

Amelia sighed.

"Yes, I suppose it was. I got annoyed by something that happened in the office and decided to go on an impulse. Rose is always saying I'm too impulsive."

They fell silent. Amelia demolished the last cake and rose.

"Thank you for the tea, Mr Milton and for rescuing me."

She said politely then added

"But I'm sure I can look after myself!"

Mr Milton's lips twitched.

"I'm sure you can. Let me get you a cab."

"Thank you, I would be grateful. I have to get back to the office. Miss Prentice will wonder where I am."

She entered the office to find a worried-looking Miss Prentice who greeted her with relief

"Mr Douglass is here, Miss Wallace. He has been waiting some time. Are you unwell?"

"No, Miss Prentice. I got delayed by the crowd going to the rally. Where is Mr Douglass?

"In your office."

Arthur was looking out of the window, his hands clasped behind his back. He turned as he heard her close the door. She was shocked to see how old he looked.

"There you are, Amelia. I was wondering what had become of you. Mr Higgins telegraphed me about this Union business so I decided to come up to town to make sure everything was under control. I have spoken to Jarvis and we have come to an agreement. Mr Higgins has all the details. I would like to be here but Eleanor is very unhappy. I don't think the treatment is doing her any good at all but Patience insists that we give it more time."

He looked closely at her.

"Is everything all right, Amelia? You look rather flushed. You're not feeling ill are you?"

"No, Arthur. I'm fine. I've just been hurrying, that's all."

"Well, look after yourself. I can't do without you!"

"I promise to be careful, Arthur. So Mrs Jarrett is no better?"

"No, I am afraid not. We are very worried about her. Nothing we can say or do seems to make any difference. She is sinking further and further into a world of her own."

He sighed.

"I see no end to it. I must go and catch my train. I promised Patience I would not be late."

After Arthur had departed Amelia tried to work but found it impossible and, for the first time since coming to work at Douglass & Co., she was pleased when the office clock showed 5.30. Perhaps she was starting a cold. When she got home she told Rose who sent her to bed with a hot drink.

In the morning she was relieved to feel her usual self and concluded that the excitement of the previous day had been to blame. She decided not to tell either Rose or Mrs Trevise about her adventure. She hoped Mr Milton would keep it to himself but perhaps she had better see if she could speak to him privately after Church on Sunday.

The next day was grey and foggy and got worse as the day wore on. By the time Bert came for her at 5.30 it was so dark and the fog so thick it was almost impossible to see and Bert expressed it as his opinion that they were 'in for it.' He had a young man with him whom he introduced as "my eldest, young Bert". Young Bert walked in front of the cab carrying a flaming torch and Bert led the horse. The fog was so dense that Amelia could not see young Bert or Bert and only the horse's hindquarters. The swirling yellow fog made her cough and she held a handkerchief over her nose and mouth. It took them longer than usual to get to Springfield Road. Several times Bert had to stop and check his direction. More than once they had near accidents as other cabs and vehicles loomed suddenly out of the fog each with a man in front carrying a flaming torch. Eventually they arrived and, as he helped her from the cab, Bert said

"If it's like this termorrer, Miss, I won't be coming out and if you take my advice you'll stay indoors."

"I will Bert, thank you. It will probably blow away by the morning."

Gloomily shaking his head Bert disappeared into the fog.

When Amelia woke the next morning, the fog was thicker than ever and true to his word, Bert did not put in an appearance. Day became night. It got into the house and, to Amy's despair, left a layer of greasy smuts on every surface. Even the food tasted of it. Mrs Trevise said it was a long time since she had seen such a fog.

Amelia spent the day doing what she most enjoyed – designing. Mrs Trevise alternately read and dozed. As Mrs Gipps had not arrived Rose and Amy spent the day in the kitchen. By the evening the fog was thicker than ever. Amelia pushed the net curtain in the drawing room aside and looked out. She could see nothing, only the fog pressed up against the window panes, even the gas street lamp outside the gate did not penetrate the gloom. Fetching a candle she held it up to the window but it was as if she looked in a mirror – only the reflection of the room behind her and herself holding the candle could be seen. The whole world had narrowed down to this one room.

Amelia and Mrs Trevise spent the evening playing Piquet while Rose read *A Tale of Two Cities.* It was very quiet, and Amelia found she was almost whispering as she announced her points and the absence of the usual noisy horse traffic passing up and down the road made the crackling of the fire sound louder than usual.

"I do hope this fog lifts soon." Mrs Trevise said "It is so depressing."

*****

There was one person and probably only one in the whole of London who was pleased to see the fog. Anderson's luck was in. His ship had been the last one up the river before the fog descended. One more day and he could have been stranded for days. He made his way slowly through the deserted streets, coughing as the yellow sulphurous fog caught in his throat. Stopping from time to time he checked his direction. Tall and broad with a lined, tanned face, he carried a large Portmanteau in his right hand, his left arm tucked into his coat. Once he cursed and put down the Portmanteau in order to rub his left arm. He muttered to himself as if he was used to spending most of his time alone.

"The sooner I find her and get away from this cursed damp the better. At least the Police are out of the way in their nice warm Station Houses."

He hesitated by the entrance to a narrow alley. A door opened in a nearby building emitting a square of light and several shadowy figures.

"The Old Kettle Drum!"

He debated whether to go in for a drink. Better not, he might be recognized even though it had been nearly ten years. He continued down the alley and into Ratcliff Court.

*****

The fog did not lift for another day by which time Amelia was impatient to get back to the office and Mrs Trevise was depressed. Only Rose and Amy seemed unaffected by their enforced imprisonment. Rose's Christmas present to Amy of a copy of Mrs Beeton's *Book of Household Management* was brought out. Amy was delighted with the gift but now confessed to Rose that her reading was not up to standard so Rose set about improving her reading skills.

On the fourth day Amelia opened her bedroom curtains to discover a clear, if somewhat misty, morning. When Bert came for her he grumbled

"Lost money I have, Miss. If I don't take the cab out I don't get paid and I don't think it 'as done Polly any good, she's wheezing something chronic." He added, worriedly.

"Polly? Is that your wife?"

"No, Miss, it's me 'orse. I can't work without an 'orse can I?"

"I'm very sorry, Bert. I hope that Polly will soon feel better."

"Thank you, Miss."

Amelia and a young boy arrived at the office entrance together.

"Are you Miss Wallace?" he piped.

"Yes – do you want to see me?"

"It's my sister, Clara" then seeing Amelia's blank expression "Clara Prentice. She's hurt herself. Walked into a wall on her way home in the fog. Mum says she won't be back until next week."

"I'm sorry to hear that. Please tell her that I hope she will soon recover."

"Thank you, Miss."

As Amelia walked through the main office, greeting and being greeted by the clerks, she pondered. Her work was almost up to date. She had trained as a Typewriter so she could do Miss Prentice's work.

Coming in from the Works several hours later, Mr Higgins was taken aback to find her at her old desk. She explained Miss Prentice's absence.

"I can manage the typewriting but I don't know shorthand, of course."

"Quite like old times, Miss Wallace."

"You never approved of Mr Douglass employing me as a Typewriter, did you, Mr Higgins?"

Amelia asked, mischievously.

"Not at first, no, but many things have changed since I first came to work for Mr Douglass. I can remember the days when…"

"Shall we make a start?"

Amelia asked, briskly. She knew that, once Mr Higgins started down memory lane there was no stopping him.

Spending the morning Typewriting reminded her of her days at Miss Gaymin's Business College and the girl she had met there – Martha Ibbotson now Martha Grayling. She had not visited her for some time and resolved that, Saturday afternoon, she would go out to the little house in the suburbs where Martha lived with her husband Albert and a brood of children. Accordingly when Bert came for her at 12.30 the next Saturday, she asked him if he could take her to Martha's.

"I'll pay the extra of course, Bert. I can't expect Mr Douglass to pay."

"It so 'appens that I'm going that way meself so there'll be no extra charge."

Bert said, comfortably.

Amelia didn't know whether to believe this statement but not wanting to offend her old friend she thanked him with a smile.

When she arrived at the terrace house Martha opened the door to her knock.

"Come in, Amelia. Go into the kitchen. I just have to go up and see to Vicky. The fog got onto her chest. She's got a dreadful cough."

"I'm sorry Martha. Never mind about me. I'll be fine. I know the way."

Amelia made her way into the kitchen. Two small boys were playing with some wooden building blocks on the hearthrug in front of the range. They looked up as she came in

"It's Aunt Amelia!" the eldest shouted and launched himself at her. She gave him a hug. His small brother was shy and hung back.

"Say hello to your Aunt, young Albert."

Amelia looked up, startled.

"James!" she said, delightedly.

James was Martha's elder brother and they had met when Amelia, who was one of Martha's bridesmaids, had spent a great deal of time with Mrs Ibbotson being fitted for her dress. Martha came from a large family. She had three sisters all married and two brothers, one in the Army and James, who still lived at home. Amelia had always liked the Ibbotson family. Her appearance seemed to make no difference to them, they simply expanded the family to include her but she had not seen a great deal of them since Martha's marriage.

"How are your Mother and Father?"

"Mother is fine and Father has just retired from the omnibuses."

"I expect he will miss them."

"Yes"

James seemed a little awkward.

Amelia tried again.

"Martha seems worried about Vicky."

"Yes, Vicky has always been delicate."

The boys resumed their play. Amelia and James watched them.

"It's a long time since I saw you." James said. "You work as a Designer I think Martha said?"

"Yes, with Douglass & Co. I'm the Chief Designer."

"Perhaps I should call you Miss Wallace but I think of you as Amelia."

"Do you think of me often?"

Amelia asked then, too late, remembered that it was not the sort of thing a young lady should say to a young man.

"Yes, I do, I…"

"Well I've managed to get Vicky off to sleep at last. Well, don't just stand there, James – get Amelia a chair!"

Martha ordered

"Sorry" James muttered.

Settling herself comfortably on a chair by the range, Martha said.

"Well, isn't this nice. You two haven't seen each other in years. Got a lot to say to each other, I expect and here's Albert at last. Now we can have our tea."

Martha chattered all through tea. When Albert did manage to get a word in he said.

"I have some news. You were engaged to Frederick Leros at one time weren't you, Amelia?"

"Yes."

"I thought so. He told me today that he is getting married."

"I hope he will be very happy." Amelia said, automatically.

She did not want to rake over old coals. Frederick had proposed to her and she had accepted him although she did not love him. When she discovered he was only marrying her to acquire a housekeeper and somebody to look after his two little girls she had broken off the engagement. It was then that she had decided she would marry for love on both sides or not at all and it looked as if it would be not at all.

James glanced at her questioningly.

"We were not suited." Amelia told him.

At that moment young Albert fell off his chair and, by the time he had been shushed and soothed with cake, it was time for the children to be put to bed. With the children settled for the night Martha proposed a game of cards. Amelia partnered James and they squabbled amicably over play. Amelia was enjoying herself and was surprised when Martha's kitchen clock struck nine.

"I must be going."

"It's late. Albert will get a cab and see you home. You can't go on your own. It's not proper for an unmarried woman to be out on her own this late."

Amelia was fond of Martha but she wished she would not keep bringing up the fact that she was married and Amelia was not.

Albert said very little until they were nearly back to Springfield Road.

"You must come and visit us more often. I know that Martha would be pleased."

Amelia promised she would. She had enjoyed herself and it had been nice to see James again.

CHAPTER SIX

Anderson sat in his rented room at the top of the three-storied terraced house forming one side of the square that was Ratcliff Court. He had some thinking to do, stimulation was needed. Going to the door he opened it and shouted down the stairs.

"Ned!"

No movement. Impatiently he shouted again, louder.

"Ned!"

There was the sound of a door slamming then booted feet on the uncarpeted wooden stairs.

"Whatcher want nah?"

"Here, take this and get me a jug of beer. And don't take all night."

Snatching the proffered coins Ned clattered away.

Grumbling to himself Anderson went back into his room, sat down at the rickety wooden table and stared at the miserable fire in the grate. He resisted the temptation to put on more coals – better not or his money would run out before he had completed what he had set out to do.

A few minutes later Ned could be heard laboriously climbing the stairs. Entering the room he placed the jug on the table. He did not speak neither did Anderson thank him. It was a ritual which had gone on regularly ever since Anderson had arrived and rented the room from Ned's father, an old acquaintance from his earlier days.

As Ned clattered back downstairs Anderson took a long swig from the jug and began to think.

First he had to find her. That would be the most difficult part. Once he had his hands on her she would never get away from him again. The best way would be through that daughter of hers. Find Rose and you found Anna. He knew where Rose had worked ten years ago. He would go there first thing in the morning. Of course, she might have left but even if she had somebody might know where she had gone. Could he take the risk? Yes, the Police would have given up looking for him years ago, he reassured himself. Besides he looked nothing like he did then. He had shaved off his moustache and his hair was now white. Only his accursed arm could give him away but then he was not the only man in London with a crippled arm. Anna would pay for what she did to him. He still had nightmares where once again he would see her coming at him with the poker. It was all Rose's fault. If she had only done as she was told and gone with him it would never have happened. He would take Anna away with him. He had every right, she was his wife and he could do what he liked with her. He went to bed and dreamt of a place in the sun waited on hand and foot by a subservient Anna.

The next morning he walked out to the suburbs where he made his way down the tree-lined roads until he came to a pair of semi-detached villas – this was it, No. 13 Belvoir Road.

He knew better than to approach the front door and going through the gate labelled "Tradesman's Entrance" knocked on the kitchen door which was opened by a smartly dressed maid.

"Not today" she said, firmly as she made to shut the door. Using his good arm he held the door open.

"I'm not selling anything. I just want some information."

The girl hesitated. Although the man looked shabby and had a crippled arm, his speech was not rough. An old soldier down on his luck perhaps.

"Information about what?"

"A girl used to work here called Rose. Black hair and green eyes."

"I don't know anything about any Rose with or without black hair and green eyes."

"I'm her father. We lost touch when I was posted abroad. I just want to know if she's alive."

A voice from inside the house invited the girl to "shut that door will you!"

Turning her head she shouted back

"I'm just coming, Mrs Deaks". Turning back to Anderson she said, hastily

"Sorry. Can't help you" and swiftly slammed the door.

A dead end. He began to walk back the way he had come then cursed as he saw a Police Officer coming towards him. Quickly thrusting his left hand into his coat pocket he smiled pleasantly saying

"Good afternoon, officer. "

"Good afternoon, Sir."

After the man had passed Inspector Burridge paused, and looked after him, thoughtfully. On his return to the Station House he went down into the basement and searched through some dusty files. Eventually he found what he was looking for. With a satisfied

"Got you, my lad!"

He took the file back to his office.

★★★★★

Anderson made his way back to Ratcliff Court. He was only mildly annoyed that he had been unsuccessful. He had a plan.

After he had partaken of the badly cooked meal provided by his landlord's wife he invited his landlord out to The Kettle Drum for a post-prandial drink where he put a proposition to him. He knew that the man dealt in second-hand clothes which involved knocking on kitchen doors and asking the servants to sell any of their employers cast-off clothing which he then sold on, at a profit, to an Old Clothes Exchange. It was a shot in the dark but it might yield fruit. Anderson proposed that, when collecting clothes, the man asked if a dark-haired, green-eyed girl called Rose worked or had worked in the house. The man had a horse and cart which would enable him to cover more ground neither would he arouse suspicion.

"Why do you want this Rose, then?"

"That's no business of yours. Will you do it or not?"

"What's in it for me?"

"Would five guineas be enough?"

"I could throw in the wife for that!"

"No thank you."

"You must want this Rose pretty bad. Girlfriend is she?"

"If you can't do the job without asking question I'll find somebody who can!"

"Sorry, Guvnor – just curious that's all" the man whined.

"Keep it to yourself or —"

"No call to get nasty!"

"Report to me tomorrow evening."

"Yes, Guvnor."

Nodding, Anderson finished his drink and left.

The next few days dragged and after a week of negative reports Anderson decided to cut his losses.

He didn't trust the man, he was probably not even enquiring about Rose so that he could make as much money as possible. It had been a bad and costly mistake.

"It's no good. I'll have to find another way. Here's your five guineas."

"Anyfink else I can do?"

"Only get out and send Ned up."

When Ned arrived Anderson gave him money for beer and told him to look sharp. By now it was dark and he lit his candle which he placed on the table. When Ned returned Anderson indicated that he was to put the jug down on the table. As Ned obeyed the light from the candle fell full on his face. Glancing at him Anderson saw that his face was bruised and scratched.

"Been in a fight, Ned?" he idly enquired.

"Yes – with a 'ell-cat."

Anderson was amused.

"What did you do to this hell-cat to make her react like that?"

"I told the truff."

"That must have been unusual for you."

Ned pulled himself up.

"I always tells the truff, Mister."

"And what was the name of this hell-cat that didn't like you telling the truth?"

"Amy. All I said was that 'er Misses 'ad an ugly face."

Anderson yawned.

"Was it that bad?"

Ned pulled down the left side of his face.

A memory stirred in Anderson's brain but he could not pin it down.

"Show me again, Ned."

Ned obliged.

"Jumped on me that Amy did. But the Missis, the one with the ugly face, was kind to me. Made me feel ashamed she did but there were no call for Amy to try and scratch me eyes aht!"

"What was the name of this ugly woman?"

"Miss Wallace. She lives with an old lady. I delivers the meat there, regular."

Wallace! It was a long shot but perhaps this Miss Wallace could lead him to Rose and through her to Anna.

Anderson tried not to sound too eager – he could be on the wrong track and he couldn't afford to throw any more money away.

"That's the only Missis there, is it?"

"No, there's Mrs Brett, the 'ousekeeper and another old lady."

"Does this Miss Wallace have black hair and green eyes?"

"Nah – but Mrs Brett does – 'ere 'ow did yer know that?"

Ned asked, suspiciously.

"Oh – just a lucky guess. Well thank you, Ned. Here's a shilling. Get yourself something for the bruises."

"Fanks – why does everyone keep givin' me money now I've bin beaten up? That Miss Wallace give me five shillin'."

Ned added, hopefully.

"Perhaps she'll give you some more if you go back before the bruises fade. Where did you say it was again?"

"Springfield Road – No. 23 – nice 'ouse. Wouldn't mind one like that meself one day."

"Well, who knows, Ned. Stranger things have happened."

Yes indeed – like spending five guineas trying to find out what was right under his nose for the price of a shilling!

★★★★★

Amelia began to make regular visits to Martha and her family. Usually James was there. Sometimes Mrs Ibbotson, Martha's mother, stayed with the children while the four of them went out to a theatre or concert but mostly they stayed in by the fire playing cards or just chatting.

All though January the weather was bitterly cold with fog and hard frosts. Bert found life difficult as the traffic was slow and the heavy frost made the cobblestones slippery. Amelia was nearly always late to the office. Frequently horses fell down sometimes breaking their legs when they would have to be shot. Amelia prayed that Polly would not suffer such a fate but Bert assured her that Polly was very sure footed and "more like a goat than an 'orse."

February was no better and people began to suffer from bad colds and fevers. Amy became ill but refused to stay in bed saying

"I'm not a weaklin'! I can do me work."

It was not until Rose pointed out that she would probably pass it on to everyone else that she finally gave in. She was scandalised when Rose insisted that she had a fire in her bedroom. When Amy protested she told her

"I nearly died once because I had no fire in my bedroom. We can't do without you, Amy, so you must get better as quickly as possible."

Amy's condition worsened and Mrs Trevise sent for the Doctor who prescribed rest and a mustard plaster.

Ned came every day to ask after Amy.

"As I was just passin' I fawt I'd just see 'ow she is."

The Doctor came several times a day and when eventually he declared Amy sufficiently recovered to sit downstairs by the kitchen range, everyone in the household breathed a sigh of relief.

Amy was not the only one struck down. Mrs Kitson became ill and Rose spent a great deal of time travelling between Springfield Road and the hotel where Mrs Kitson stayed.

"I do wish your mother would come and stay here, Rose. It is so tiring for you and I'm sure she would be more comfortable."

Mrs Trevise said one day as Rose dropped, exhausted, on to the drawing room sofa.

"She is too ill to move at the moment, Madam but, as soon as she is better I'll do my best to persuade her to come."

Rose promised.

At Douglass's half the workforce were sick including Mr Higgins and Miss Prentice. Amelia was doing not only Mr Higgins' work but Miss Prentice's also and fitting her own work in between. She arrived home exhausted. It was difficult trying to keep up with John's demands for new designs and she frequently fell asleep over her sketch pad only to wake, cold and aching in the early hours. She longed for the Spring and counted the days until March. But when it came, March was no better with fog, heavy snowfalls and even colder weather. She managed to struggle to work through it all and was delighted when Mr Higgins returned, especially as Miss Prentice was still away.

When Winter, finally and with great reluctance, loosened its grip, Miss Prentice returned, thinner and paler and things returned to normal.

During the Winter, Rose, assisted by Amy, who had revealed a flare for dressmaking, had made Amelia an entire wardrobe. When Amelia protested that she had enough clothes Rose took no heed only saying

"I've some blue silk put by, it will make up into a lovely dress."

One Saturday morning late in March, Amelia hurried home. As soon as she saw Rose she told her

"I'm meeting Martha and Albert and we are going for a walk in the Park. James will be here soon to fetch me."

Rose was delighted.

"It's a lovely warm day. Just the day to wear the new blue silk. I'll get it out shall I?"

Amelia protested that she would not have time to change.

"Surely you don't intend going out in your working dress! You must make an effort, Amelia!"

"I don't see why. Nobody will want to look at me!" Amelia said, bitterly.

"There will be no more talk like that if you please, Miss. Now come along or you will be late."

Once in her bedroom Amelia removed her skirt and blouse while Rose took the blue silk dress from the wardrobe and placed it carefully on the bed. Then, telling Amelia she had something for her, she went into her own room and returned carrying what looked like half a large birdcage.

"Oh no, Rose!" Amelia stepped back in horror. "I'm not wearing that! I'll never be able to sit down! The pad I wear to work will do just as well."

"It will not do, Amelia. This is a proper bustle. It is the latest thing. It has springs so…"

"SPRINGS!"

"So that it can fold up when you sit down and it is very light, you won't know you're wearing it. Just try it and see what you think." Rose wheedled.

"Well…"

"Good, but first come here and let me re-tie your stays."

As Rose pulled on the laces Amelia gasped

"Perhaps one day women won't wear stays!"

Rose paused, shocked.

"Of course respectable women will always wear stays! Whatever next!" and tugged harder.

Once she was satisfied that Amelia had the smallest waist that could be contrived she helped her first into her under petticoat and then the bustle. Amelia expected it to be heavy but it was very light. She tried sitting on the bedroom chair and, sure enough, it folded up. In fact she found it very comfortable.

Rose watched her.

"Well?"

"Yes, it is comfortable and it does fold up. I suppose it would do no harm to wear it."

Amelia grudgingly admitted.

After Rose had helped her into her petticoat and dress Amelia studied herself in her wardrobe mirror. She had to admit that the fitted bodice with its standing collar and long tight sleeves together with the fullness at the back of the skirt emphasized by the bustle was a far cry from her usual working dress of plain black skirt and white blouse.

"Do you think the earrings Mama gave me will go with this dress?" Amelia asked.

Opening a jewel case on the dressing table Rose took out the sapphire and diamond cluster earrings and handed them to Amelia who, after placing them in her ears, looked in the mirror to see the effect.

Rose stood back in admiration.

"You *do* look elegant, Amelia. Here is your bonnet."

She helped to adjust the matching blue silk bonnet complete with an ostrich feather round the brim and tied the velvet ties under Amelia's chin.

When Amelia came carefully down the stairs to where James was waiting in the hall, she was taken aback when he said

"You look lovely, Amelia."

As she smiled at the compliment she reflected on what a difference a few fine feathers made! Later, walking down the road on James's arm and shielding her face with her white lace parasol she felt every inch the fine lady.

Meeting the rest of the party at the park gates they entered and mingled with the leisurely crowd making its way to the bandstand where uniformed bandsmen were playing selections from Gilbert and Sullivan. As Amelia sank into her deckchair she remembered the last time she had come into the park with a man. It had been with Frederick Leros. Then she reproached herself for indulging in unpleasant memories on such a lovely afternoon.

After they had listened to the band for some time James leaned towards her and said

"Would you like to walk, Amelia?"

Amelia found that, for some reason, she did not want to be alone with James.

"I don't think we should, James. It would look very rude."

James sighed

"Very well. But I was hoping to speak to you alone."

"Perhaps another day."

Getting up Martha picked up the youngest boy.

"I'm gasping. Lets find some tea. Don't go running off, Vicky."

She admonished as Vicky, blonde curls bobbing, began to skip along in front.

Amelia took young Albert's hand and they all made their way to the tea tent which had been erected near the lake. It was pleasant sitting in the shade sipping tea and eating dainty cakes.

They were all enjoying the tea and conversation when Martha suddenly asked

"Where's Vicky?"

"Don't worry, she can't be far. She was here just a minute ago."

Albert soothed. They looked all round the tent but there was no sign of the little girl.

"She likes ducks."Young Albert remarked.

"The lake!" Martha screamed.

As one they ran out of the tent in the direction of the lake.The two men easily outstripping the women who were encumbered with their skirts plus two small children. Martha and Amelia arrived, panting, at the lakeside to see Albert wading to the side of the lake carrying a dripping and howling Vicky.

"She fell in just as I got here." He explained.

Albert handed Vicky over to her mother who promptly smacked her which made her howl even louder, her brothers joining in.

"We must get her home and into a hot bath." Albert shouted above the din.

"I'll take Amelia home." James said, taking Amelia's arm.

"I do hope Vicky doesn't catch cold." Amelia said as they left the park.

"She was more frightened than anything and it is a warm day. Now we are alone there is something I want to ask you, Amelia. We get on well together, don't we?"

"Yes, we do. I like your family, James. They have always been kind to me."

"How would you like to become part of my family?"

Amelia stopped dead in her tracks. A man walked into her and apologized. Amelia did not see or hear him.

"What do you mean?"

"Will you marry me, Amelia? I'm doing very well in the office and I have every intention of one day becoming Chief Clerk and that would mean a salary of £100 per annum!" he said, impressively.

When Amelia did not respond but resumed walking he continued.

"Obviously as a married woman you will not be able to continue working. We might be able to afford a servant later on, though."

Amelia was trying to sort out her emotions. Shock, disbelief, and, surprisingly, irritation. She would have to think this over.

By now they had arrived at Springfield Road.

"I can't give you an answer now, James. I need time to think."

"Of course, I understand, but don't take too long."

Amy opening the door at that moment saved Amelia from replying. Lifting his hat politely, James departed.

Amelia did not hear Amy's chatter as she took her bonnet and parasol. She was distracted for the rest of the evening and only answered in monosyllables when Rose asked her if she had enjoyed her outing. Certain Amelia was sickening for a summer cold, Rose packed her off early to bed where Amelia lay thinking until she fell asleep, exhausted.

CHAPTER SEVEN

The next morning Amelia woke with a pounding headache and no nearer a solution. All through April and May she considered her options. She knew this would be her one and only chance of a home and family but she also knew she did not love James. She was very fond of him but that was not the same thing. She badly wanted to discuss the problem with Rose but they never seemed to be alone. Amelia considered consulting Sophia but knew she would immediately ask John for his opinion and she felt she could do without one of John's lectures.

In spite of her worries Amelia was amused to see that, once it was established that Mrs Kitson was a wealthy woman, the social barriers came down so far as Sophia was concerned and she treated not only Mrs Kitson but also Rose as an equal. The three of them made frequent shopping trips to Gamages or Marshal and Snelgrove after which they usually returned to Springfield Road for tea.

As Mrs Kitson was such a frequent visitor to Springfield Road, Rose, Sophia and Mrs Trevise all tried to persuade her to take up Mrs Trevise's invitation to stay but she was adamant.

"I think it is best if I stay at the hotel. Soon Rose and I will begin looking for a house."

Realizing they could not move her the ladies went back to their heated discussion regarding the merits of the "Home Friend" magazine over "Cassell's Family Magazine."

Amelia became more and more depressed. From time to time James asked her for a decision but she always evaded the question. She knew things could not continue in this way and when, by July, she still had not given him an answer he became impatient.

"Why are you so reluctant to give me an answer, Amelia? I don't understand why you are taking so long. I have been very patient so far. I know you will marry me in the end so why not say so? Are you being modest? If so I think you have taken modesty far enough."

"No, James, I am not being modest."

"What is it then? Is there something about me that you would like me to change? I'll do anything."

"No, it is nothing to do with you, it is to do with me. I don't seem to be able to think at the moment and it is a very important decision. It affects the rest of my life."

James realized it would do no good to press her. He would just have to take action himself.

The weather had turned sultry and a thick yellow fog hung in the air – the product of countless household fires. One foggy Saturday afternoon Mrs Kitson came to tea. As Amy helped her off with her cloak and bonnet Mrs Kitson began to cough. A glass of water was produced and Rose helped her to a chair. Seeing her mother finding it difficult to catch her breath Rose became alarmed. Mrs Trevise summoned her Doctor. After he had made his examination he asked Rose if he could see her in private. Making sure her mother was comfortably settled on the drawing room sofa, Rose went outside.

"Is she very ill, Doctor?"

"I'm afraid so and these dreadful fogs do not help her condition. She needs very careful nursing. I'll leave you some medicine and will come back tomorrow."

When Rose re-entered the sitting room her mother smiled at her.

"Don't look so alarmed Rose. I can guess what the Doctor told you. The Doctor in Edinburgh told me the same thing. That's why I had to come and find you, before it was too late."

Before Rose could reply Mrs Trevise came into the room asking "What did the Doctor say?"

"Only what I already knew. He has left me some medicine."

"He says mother must have careful nursing, Mrs Trevise, so I am going back to her hotel to look after her."

"Why don't you stay here, Mrs Kitson. It would be much nicer than the hotel and we have plenty of room."

"I don't know. It's very good of you, Mrs Trevise, but it would be a great deal of trouble and Rose can just as easily look after me at the hotel."

"Well stay until you feel better. The fog is getting thicker you know." Mrs Trevise said, anxiously.

Mrs Kitson closed her eyes, wearily.

"Perhaps it would be wise but only until I feel strong enough to travel."

"That's settled then. Rose, you and Amy get the room next to yours ready and I'll stay with your mother until she is able to go to bed. Make sure Amy airs the sheets."

Once they were alone Mrs Trevise said

"Do think over my offer. I would be delighted to have you here as my guest. The hotel might refuse to let you stay and your only alternative then would be to go to the hospital which I'm sure you have no wish to do."

They both knew that hospital was generally considered to be the place you went to die and most people resisted entering it as long as they were able.

"No, indeed. Thank you. I'll think it over."

"Good – ah, here is Rose to help you up to bed."

Amelia saw even less of Rose who spent every spare moment with her mother. Upon the Doctor pronouncing her well enough to sit downstairs Mrs Kitson insisted on helping with the never ending supply of collars and cuffs to be replaced after laundering; the unpicking and resewing of clothes after cleaning, and the turning of dresses when faded. July turned into August and it was taken for granted that Mrs Kitson would remain as a permanent member of the household much to everyone's relief.

At the beginning of August, Mrs Trevise, as was her habit, rented a seaside villa on the South Coast for the month. Mrs Gipps was given a month's wages and Amy was to accompany them. They were happily discussing what clothes they would take.

"If you tell me what you want packed, Amelia, I can do it for you." Rose offered.

"But I'm staying here." Amelia replied.

"Of course you are coming. You always come away with us."

"We are just beginning on plans for the Christmas trade, Rose. With Arthur away I'm in charge. Mr Higgins can't possibly manage on his own."

She didn't want to go away, she wanted to go to work where she could lose herself in her designing and push decision making to the back of her mind.

Rose said no more but, when she and Sophia were sitting in Lyons having tea after an afternoon spent shopping for holiday necessities, she told her that Amelia had refused to go and she was worried about her staying in the house on her own.

"If Amelia has made up her mind not to go nothing you can say will change her mind. She is more like John than she realizes. But, I agree with you, it's not proper for a young woman to stay in the house on her own. Goodness knows how she would manage. I think I have a solution. Suppose we put it to her that, either she goes with you or she comes to stay with me?"

"That would be an ideal solution, Mrs Wallace. Perhaps we could tell her together this evening?"

Having settled the problem of Amelia the two ladies went on to the more pressing matter of how many pairs of boots and shoes would be necessary and whether Rose needed evening slippers of satin or if white kid would be more sensible for a month's stay in a seaside resort.

Mrs Trevise was apprised of the plan so that, upon the ultimatum being put to her, Amelia found she was no match for three determined ladies and agreed to go and stay at No.13. Secretly she was quite relieved as she had not relished the thought of being on her own and having to fend for herself.

She had refused several of Martha's invitations, pleading pressure of work but she knew this could not continue.

One evening when Amelia, exhausted from a frustrating day of battling with Mr Higgins over the cost of materials, returned to Belvoir Road, she was informed by Elsie, the maid, that

"The Master said you were to go to his study as soon as you came in, Miss Wallace."

Amelia sighed. She was getting tired of John's autocratic ways. She almost considered ignoring the summons but she was too tired to put up with the consequent furore if she did not immediately comply. She entered the study without knocking.

John looked up from the desk and, for a split second, she saw her father.

"There you are, Amelia."

"You have something you wish to speak to me about, John? I am rather tired."

"This can't wait. Sit down."

She sat down on the chair in front of the desk. John rose and took up his favourite stance in front of the empty grate. She knew from bitter experience that this was not a good sign.

"I had a visitor at the Works today."

What could that possibly have to do with her, she wondered. When Amelia did not respond he asked

"Do you know who it was?"

"Of course not, John. Do tell me what all this is about."

"My visitor was James Ibbotson."

"James!"

"You had no idea he was going to call on me?"

"No, I can't think why he should be calling on you. He doesn't even know you."

"But he knows you, does he not? I see by your face that I am right. Perhaps you can guess why he came?"

Amelia shook her head, but had a horrible presentiment.

"He had the impertinence to ask if I would consent to your marriage. Have you engaged yourself to this person without my consent, Amelia?"

"He has proposed but I have not given him my answer."

"And you did not think it incumbent upon you to inform me, your male guardian, of the fact? You will tell him that you refuse his offer. It appears that he is a *Clerk* in an *Insurance Office* and his father is a retired *omnibus driver*!"

John made it sound as if Mr Ibbotson Snr was a retired Jack Ketch, the public hangman.

"They are very nice people. They have been kind to me."

"Of course they have. Think what is at stake – marriage to the sister of one of the most important business men in London!"

Drawing himself up John grasped himself by the coat lapels. Amelia thought he looked ridiculous.

"I have not yet decided to marry James, but, if I decide to accept his proposal I shall marry him whether you like it or not!"

Amelia replied, defiantly.

John went a very nasty shade of purple and so far forgot himself as to place his hands on the arms of Amelia's chair and thrust his face into hers.

"I'll tell you what I told him, that, if you marry him without my consent, I'll disown you. Don't you realize that he is only after your money?" His voice rose. "Look in a mirror – how could it be otherwise!"

Seeing Amelia go white with shock he realized he had gone too far. Going back to the hearthrug he said, in what he considered to be a conciliatory tone.

"I'm sorry, Amelia, but it is the truth. Better to face it, and reconcile yourself to the fact that you are never going to get married. Don't worry, you will always have a home here. Now tell me you will refuse this offer and we will say no more about it."

Instead of replying Amelia jumped up and ran from the room not stopping until she was in her bedroom, where she slammed the door with such force that the wall shook. She began to pace up and down.

"How dare he!" she ranted, kicking an inoffensive stool out of her way. She was not quite sure which man she meant – James for daring to go behind her back or John for giving her orders on how to conduct her life. For a row of pins she would marry James to spite John. Even as she formed the thought she knew she would do no such thing. She sat down on the edge of the bed. What *was* she to *do*?

She was very silent all through dinner and, upon Sophia enquiring if she was feeling quite well, replied,

"I've got rather a bad headache, Mama. I think I'll go to bed."

"That would be best. You are probably overtired. Soak a handkerchief in eau-de-cologne and put it on your forehead." Sophia advised.

"Yes, Mama. Good night. Good night, John."

"Good night, Amelia. Have a good night's rest and you will feel calmer in the morning."

Amelia did not reply. She sat for hours by her open window, looking out over the roofs of London and thinking. She remembered how, when she was young, she had vowed to herself she would only marry for love. But that was when she was young. Now she was conscious of time running out. She would never get another chance. By the morning she still had not come to a decision.

To her dismay she remembered that she had accepted an invitation to tea with all the Ibbotson family to mark the occasion of James's elder brother, Henry, a sergeant in the Army, going overseas to Africa. She did not see how she could refuse as Mrs Ibbotson had made a special point of asking her. She consoled herself with the thought that there would be plenty of people there. It should not be too difficult to avoid being alone with James.

Everything went as she had hoped. All the family made her welcome and she managed to avoid James. She thought Henry looked very handsome in his uniform. He expressed his intention of "giving the Boers something to remember me by!" When the time came for him to leave the entire family went out to wave him off down the street. As they all trooped back into the house, James walked determinedly in Amelia's direction.

"Has your brother told you what happened when I went to see him?"

"Yes, he has. You should not have spoken to him before I had given you my answer."

"I am tired of waiting, Amelia. I had to do something. Your brother seems to think I only want your money. I don't want your money, Amelia. I want you. Why can't you give me an answer? Surely you know whether you love me or not?"

"I'm not sure, James. I'm sorry."

"Even if you don't love me now I'm sure you will once we are married and you are away from the influence of that brother of yours."

"I can't talk here, James. I'll give you an answer but I need more time."

"Time! You've had plenty of time. It's not fair to..."

"I must go and help your mother." Amelia made her escape.

She found Mrs Ibbotson standing looking out of the scullery window. Hearing Amelia come into the room she turned and Amelia was shocked to see tears streaming down her face.

"Oh, its you, Amelia."

"Whatever is the matter, Mrs Ibbotson?"

"It's silly I know but I have a dreadful feeling I shall never see Henry alive again."

"Shall I fetch May?" May was Mrs Ibbotson's eldest daughter.

"No, at least not yet. I want to talk to you, Amelia. It's about James."

"Yes?"

"He has told me that he has proposed to you. He is anxious for an answer. It's not right to keep him in suspense. He loves you, Amelia.

We would all be delighted to welcome you into the family. Do you love James?"

Amelia did not answer.

"You must be absolutely sure, Amelia. Marriage is not easy you know. If you are not sure you must refuse him. Better for him to be made unhappy now than after you are married."

"I know I have been unfair to James but it's just that…"

"You think you will never get another chance. I do understand, Amelia, but my main concern is my son's happiness. The decision is yours, Amelia. All I ask is that you let James have an answer soon."

"Yes, I promise I'll give him an answer by the end of the week. Now I think I had better go home."

"Will you ask May to come in – we have a great deal of clearing up to do."

Amelia, Martha, Alfred and the three children were to share a Hackney.

As he handed her into the cab James asked

"When, Amelia?"

"On Saturday. Meet me in the Park on Saturday afternoon."

He nodded then stood watching the cab until it was swallowed up in the traffic.

"Have you two love-birds had a quarrel?" Martha asked, archly.

"No."

Martha opened her mouth to continue and Alfred hastily said

"I think Vicky is going to be sick."

Once she was back at Belvoir Road, Amelia, pleading a headache, went straight to her room.

Sophia was worried and expressed her concern to John.

"I can't think what is the matter with Amelia. I hope she isn't going to be ill."

"She will get over it, Mother."

"Get over what, John? What has happened?"

"Amelia was about to make an unfortunate marriage which would have forced me, as head of the family, to disown her and forbid her the house."

"In what way unfortunate, John?"

"I have dealt with the matter, Mother and do not intend to discuss it further. Now I have some work to do in my study."

Sophia watched him leave the room. Sometimes she found her son's overbearing ways almost intolerable. If only William were still alive. He would have known exactly how to deal with Amelia without arousing her independent spirit. She thought of speaking to Amelia herself but, in the end, decided against it. She knew how prickly her youngest daughter could be if she thought her freedom to conduct her own affairs was being threatened. Really life was very difficult!

Amelia badly needed some one to talk to. Everything kept going round in her head. She tried to put her thoughts into some sort of order. What would be the consequences if she married James? She had no doubt that John would carry out his threat to disown her. His pride would not allow him to do otherwise. James had made it quite clear that he would expect her to give up her work. Where would they live? She realized that, on James's low salary she could not have the life style she was used to. There would be no cook, probably only one servant and, inevitably, children to provide for. But they could be happy together. James was a kind man. She was sure he would never ill-treat her and she got on well with his family. On the other hand, if she did not marry him she would be able to continue with the work she loved, although, when she could no longer work she would become a dependent. John had said she would always have a home with him but what if he married again? His second wife could be like the first and refuse to have her in the house.

She hesitated to ask her mother's advice much as she would have liked to do so. She would only insist on bringing John into the discussion and he had already made his position clear. Had John told Mama about his interview with James? If only she could talk to somebody. Somebody outside the family. Somebody who had no interest in her decision one way or the other.

She was sure that never, in the entire history of the world, had a week gone with such speed. She was so absorbed in her problem that she did not notice when people stopped speaking to her at the office as she either snapped at them or did not answer. Mr Higgins and Miss Prentice discussed the matter and decided it was something to do with the current design in which case it would be best to leave her alone to sort out the problem in her own way.

Saturday arrived and no concrete decision had been made. Sometimes she decided one way only to change her mind and decide on the alternative switching back several hours later. She was not due to meet James until later in the afternoon. She found she could not stay indoors so went out for a walk in the hope that it would clear her head. After a time she found herself outside St. Mary's and on impulse went inside.

It was cool and quiet. She sank down on a pew and let the peace flow over her. Surely in such a place the answer would come?

CHAPTER EIGHT

Anderson's plans were slowly taking shape. It had taken many months of patient groundwork. When his money ran out he obtained the post of Verger and Pew Opener at his local Church – St. George's-in-the-East. He acquainted himself with every nook and cranny of the building and made sure he was seen coming and going at all hours of the day and night. After several months the Vicar entrusted him with the keys to the Church. When the Bishop made his annual visit the Vicar introduced him to the Bishop with the words

"Anderson, My Lord, my right-hand man. Totally indispensable."

Now all Anderson had to do was to be patient. He would know when the time was right and then he would strike.

*****

In the cool of the Church Amelia tried to pray but, for some reason, prayer would not come. Perhaps she was tired. She sat back and closed her eyes.

"Miss Wallace? Are you quite well?"

Opening her eyes she saw Mr Milton bending over her, solicitously.

"Quite well, thank you, Mr Milton."

"You seem troubled. Can I help?"

"I don't think so."

"Are you sure? Perhaps if you talk about whatever it is that is making you frown so ferociously it might help. Is there trouble at home?"

"No, I really don't think…"

"I'm old enough to be your elder brother and I'm very discreet."

Amelia found this concept novel and, before she could think burst out with

"But you are nothing like my brother! He's pompous and arrogant and you're just – nice!"

Mr Milton coughed and said

"Thank you, Amelia. I may call you Amelia, may I not?"

"Of course – you are my elder brother after all!"

"Now you are smiling again, tell me, what is the matter?"

Sitting down in the pew in front he leaned his arms on the back.

"Well… I've received a proposal of marriage."

She said, in a rush.

He looked startled then recovered and said

"Congratulations. When is the wedding to take place?"

"That's the trouble – I don't know whether to accept the proposal or not."

"The most important question is, do you love the young man?"

"No, but I'm very fond of him. We have known each other for a long time. I do so want a husband and children like other women. Perhaps I would love him in time – he seems to think so."

"You have told him that you don't love him?"

"Not in so many words. He would be so hurt that I can't. I shall never get another chance to be married if I refuse James. I promised to give him my answer this afternoon – what can I tell him?"

Amelia was almost in tears. Mr Milton was silent for some time then he said

"Only you can decide, Amelia. It is hard I know but I am sure you will make the right decision. I will leave you to your thoughts."

"Thank you, Mr Milton.

He nodded and walked away towards the vestry.

★★★★★

Amelia was late getting to the meeting place. James was already there, pacing back and forth. His face lit up when he saw her.

"I thought you had decided not to come. Well, what is your answer?"

"I can't marry you, James. I don't love you."

"But I'm sure you will in time. You don't hate me do you?"

"Of course not. I'm very fond of you but..."

"There you are then, that's settled. You've made me very happy, Amelia. When shall we be married? We must tell our families. I know your brother will be angry but perhaps he will come round in time. Martha will be..."

"STOP! STOP!"

In her agitation Amelia pulled on his arm. When she had his attention she drew a deep breath and said, very slowly and firmly.

"I am not going to marry you, James. I'm sorry if anything I have done or said has led you to think otherwise. It would not be right as I can't love you as a wife should love her husband. I'm sorry."

James went white with fury.

"Is that all you have to say – you're sorry! You're like that brother of yours – you don't think I'm good enough for you, do you? I thought better of you, Amelia but I see you are like the rest of your class – when it comes to the point you all stick together!"

"I think I should like to go home now, James." Amelia said, stiffly.

They walked back to No.13 in silence and in silence they parted.

Several times over the next few days Amelia nearly confided in Sophia but always the thought of John's self-satisfaction at the thought that she had taken his advice stopped her.

Several times over the next few days Sophia nearly asked Amelia if the reason why she looked so pale and hardly ate was to do with the proposal of marriage she had received and John's reaction to it. She was longing to know what Amelia had decided to do but she knew that Amelia would not take kindly to what she would regard as interference. If she wanted to talk to her or ask her advice she would. Both longed to talk to the other about what was uppermost in their minds but neither had the courage to face possible rejection.

Amelia was relieved when September came and she was able to return to Springfield Road.

Everyone seemed better for the holiday. Amy especially. She had filled out and was turning into a very good looking young woman. A transformation which, according to Rose, had not escaped the notice of various under footmen and tradesmen's assistants.

"I had to tell her that followers were not allowed in the kitchen." Rose told Amelia.

Amy never tired of talking about the wonderful time she had had.

"I ain't never before seen the sea, Miss." She informed Amelia as she knelt making up the fire in the drawing room.. "It's that big you would never believe. And the sand – you can make castles and things out of it. Did you know that? Mrs Trevise let me 'ave every afternoon off and I 'ad that many fellas." She sighed, ecstatically.

"I'm pleased you enjoyed yourself, Amy. Won't you miss all your admirers?"

"Oh no, Miss. To tell you the truth" – she lowered her voice, conspiratorially. "I already 'ave a young man 'ere."

She paused, expectantly fire tongs in hand. Amelia dutifully raised her eyebrows.

"Yes, Miss – Ned! 'e's my steady."

"Does Ned know this?"

"Not yet, Miss, but 'e will."

Amy replied, cheerfully as she put the coal on the fire, got to her feet and left the room.

Amelia sighed, she envied her, so young, so pretty and so sure of her power to attract.

The following Saturday afternoon, Amelia set out to visit Martha. She was surprised when, upon opening the door and seeing who was on the doorstep, Martha sniffed and said, coldly

"Oh, it's you. I suppose you'd better come in."

Puzzled, Amelia followed her into the kitchen.

Martha did not ask her to sit down. She stood, with arms folded, looking Amelia up and down then said

"I'm surprised you have the nerve to show your face round here!"

"Why, whatever is the matter, Martha?"

"As if you don't know! James is really upset."

Amelia began to understand.

"I am sorry Martha but I am sure it is for the best."

"Oh yes – best for you and your stuck-up family I don't doubt! James told us all about his interview with your brother. Treating him like one of his workmen! We've never been good enough for you have we? Now James is talking about joining the Army and going to Africa with Henry. If he gets killed it will be all your fault!" she ended, dramatically.

"*We* can still be friends, Martha, can't we?" Amelia pleaded.

Albert had entered the room during Martha's tirade and now tried to calm her down.

"It's nothing to do with us, Martha. It's between James and Amelia. Naturally, as Amelia's friend you are disappointed, but if Amelia doesn't want to marry James that's the end of it."

Ignoring him Martha continued to glare at Amelia.

"Friends – how can we be friends now? And why don't you want to marry my brother? Not likely to be asked again are you? It was good of James to offer to take on an ugly wife. Not many men would."

Martha said, venomously.

Albert gasped and Martha put a hand over her mouth.

"Martha!" Albert exclaimed in shocked tones.

"I didn't mean… I'm upset."

White-faced, Amelia did not reply but turned on her heel and left the house.

Half way down the road Albert caught up with her.

"Let me get a cab and take you home."

Amelia was inclined to refuse but commonsense told her she could not walk all the way home and she was too upset to take the omnibus and submit herself to the inevitable stares so she let him hail a passing cab.

"I'm sorry that Martha spoke to you like that." Albert said, once they were on their way.

"She is not a vicious person but she was so looking forward to having you as a sister-in-law. She had made all sorts of plans about the outings you would have together. I know it's no excuse but she is very fond of you and James."

"I won't say that I'm not very hurt, Albert but I just could not marry James. It had nothing to do with my family. I make my own decisions."

"Of course, but I shouldn't come round again if I were you – at least not for a while."

Amelia did not reply and they finished the journey in silence.

Amelia was extremely hurt. She had always liked Martha but, since her marriage, she seemed to have changed. If that is what marriage does to you, she thought, I'm better without it.

John became very demanding and more and more of her spare time was taken up with his designs. She was finding it difficult to come up with new ideas and spent long hours at her desk. Rose became concerned as she saw Amelia becoming thinner with permanent dark rings under her eyes. When she tried to find out what was troubling her, Amelia would only irritably reply that she wished everyone would leave her alone to get on with her life in her own way.

Amelia knew Rose was worried about her but was too hurt and upset to talk about it even to Rose. She woke in the early hours with the same question going round in her mind – had she done the right thing? Then she would tell herself, sternly, that, yes, she had, then, sitting up in bed, she would begin to sketch a design.

In October a thick black fog descended. Mrs Kitson was confined to bed with a cough, Polly wheezed and Amelia was late for work which made her more irritable than ever. On one of Arthur's rare visits he asked her if anything was wrong.

"Higgins and Miss Prentice are worried about you, Amelia."

"Why can't people mind their own business!" Amelia snapped.

"It is their business. You are not communicating with them let alone co-operating. This is a business and it is not run for your convenience. If the work is becoming too much for you, and I must say some of your designs do not come up to your usual standard, perhaps you should think about leaving."

As he had hoped Amelia was shocked into speech.

"I'm sorry, Arthur. I know I have not been very nice to anyone lately. I've had a great deal on my mind but I promise to make an effort. I don't want to leave."

"I don't want you to leave either but you must remember how important you are to the business. If we don't have good popular designs we won't sell our products which means there will be a loss of trade and that, together with the competition from France, could well be the end of us."

Arthur wondered, not for the first time, whether employing a woman had been a good idea after all. He knew they didn't have the same staying power as men. Perhaps Amelia had reached the end of her productive life. He had enough problems in his private life without problems with the business.

Amelia was considerably shaken. She had taken it for granted that she would continue to work for Arthur until she decided the time had come to stop.

There was only one person in whom she felt she could confide – Mr Milton. She supposed it was because he was a Vicar and used to listening to people's troubles. She had got into the habit of talking to him on a Sunday after the Morning Service while she waited for the others to collect their bags and cloaks and chat to their friends. He had asked her what her decision had been regarding James's proposal. When she told him she had rejected him and also Martha's reaction to the news he had only said

"I'm sure you've done the right thing."

"Thank you for all your help. It's good to have somebody I can talk to who will listen and not try and tell me what to do."

"I'm sure they are only trying to help, Amelia. I have a friend who runs a mission in one of the poorer districts of London. He is the Vicar in charge of St Georges-in-the-East. He has asked me if I could help to provide toys for the children for Christmas. Do you think Mr Douglass would be willing to donate some toys?"

"I'll ask him. I'm sure he would be very pleased to do so. I am working on a design at the moment. It's a clockwork mouse that can run along the floor."

"It sounds the ideal thing for boys who want to frighten their sisters."

"And for the girls a doll that can crawl across the floor. Then there is a ship that, when it is put down onto a flat surface, will seem to float up and down as if it is on water. Oh! and also a…"

"And you designed all these toys?"

"Oh, yes."

"You love your work, don't you Amelia?"

"Yes, I do."

"Had you married James would he have been willing to let you continue?"

"Oh no, he said he would feel humiliated if his wife worked – it would look as if he could not afford to keep her."

"So now you are able to continue to do the work you love and also bring happiness to children both rich and poor."

"Yes – I see what you mean. I should be grateful that there is something I can do to make these children's lives better and also something I enjoy doing. So I should stop feeling sorry for myself and making everyone's life a misery over something that can never be."

"Not that you can see at the moment. You never know what is round the corner."

"That's what Rose says."

"Rose is a very sensible woman. Now I must go and talk to Mrs Fleming. She has been looking in this direction for some time."

Amelia's family and work colleagues were surprised and pleased to find that she had returned to her old self in spite of the dark foggy November days and long nights. She threw herself into her designs and, on Arthur's next visit, asked him about donating some of the toys to the mission.

"Of course, Amelia. You and Higgins arrange it between you. But don't give away our entire stock will you!"

On Christmas Eve Amelia watched the loading of the wagon taking the toys to the mission.

"Perhaps I should come too, Mr. Higgins."

"No, Miss Wallace – it is far too rough for a respectable woman. I'll take Jarvis and three of the men. We don't want the toys stolen before the children even see them although I doubt they will be allowed to keep them for very long."

"Why shouldn't they keep them? They are a gift!"

"Their fathers will probably sell them to pay for drink, Miss Wallace." Then, seeing the dismay on her face "but I expect the children will have got tired of them by then, you know what children are."

Never having had a great deal to do with children Amelia didn't know but presumed Mr. Higgins, the father of eleven, did.

"Very well, Mr. Higgins. I leave it to you."

★★★★★

It was Christmas Eve and at St Georges the Rev. Hendry was surrounded by eager children as he handed out toys, aided by his Verger.

"These are very fine toys, Anderson. Mr Milton tells me they were designed by a woman – can you believe it!"

"Really, Sir? And what would be this woman's name?"

"I have no idea. Now, Lizzie, don't push, there is plenty for everyone."

Anderson peered at the name on the boxes – Douglass & Co. – woman designer – the ugly one! Why did she keep haunting him?

★★★★★

Later that day, Edmund sat in the study of his friend Joseph Hendry, the incumbent of St. Georges-in-the-East. They had just finished a splendid dinner and were now drinking some excellent port wine and discussing Joseph's plans to open a Mission for the poor people of the Parish.

"I should be very pleased to help in any way I can" Edmund said. "Although, at the moment I can't see how."

"It will all become clear once we begin in earnest."

"You are going to stay in London then? I thought you wanted to have a country Parish?"

"Eventually. Abigail doesn't care to live in London, especially in a Parish like this."

"Surely if this is where you are called she will have no objection?"

"As the daughter of a Minor Canon of Worcester Cathedral you can't expect her to be happy here." Joseph admonished.

"No, I suppose not."

Edmund agreed. He had long ago realized that Joseph was what he privately called a "professional Clergyman". He had no doubt that, one day, he would become a Bishop.

"And you, Edmund. Are you going to stay in London all your life?"

"I'm not sure that I'm going to remain a clergyman, Joseph."

Joseph sat up.

"Oh, what would you do?"

"I've been thinking lately that I would like to do something for underprivileged boys. Give them a start in life, but it is only an idea at the moment."

"In my experience the poor never appreciate what you do for them, Edmund, and you can't expect it, it isn't in their nature."

Edmund thought it best to change the subject.

"Did you appoint a Verger?"

"Oh yes. A very reliable man. Widower, no children. Lives locally. Works very hard, is here all hours of the day and night. Knows the Church buildings better than I do. In fact, I have given him the Church keys."

"Was that wise, Joseph?"

"I don't see why not. He seems a better class of person than you usually find in this area."

"What do you know of his background?"

"Apparently he was an officer in the Army. Got wounded. He has a badly mishapen arm but seems to manage with it well enough."

"I should be careful, Joseph."

"No need I do assure you. Do you have any plans to get married, Edmund? No Bishop's daughter tucked away somewhere?"

Edmund found this remark distasteful.

"No, Joseph. When I marry I shall marry for love, not advantage."

"Oh tush! That is just romantic nonsense! A wife with good connections and a pleasing appearance is an asset to any man, clergyman or not."

"I can't agree with you, Joseph."

"Have you anyone in mind?"

"No – well, not exactly."

"Do I hear a note of doubt? Has some pretty young thing caught your eye as you looked down from your pulpit one Sunday morning?"

"Of course not, Joseph.

Edmund glanced at the clock on the mantelpiece.

"I must go. Thank you for the dinner."

"My pleasure. Now let me see you out. I expect my housekeeper, has gone to bed."

As Edmund journeyed home he knew that, at some point during the conversation, he had made up his mind not to remain a Parish Priest.

*****

Christmas at Springfield Road was very merry. Mrs Kitson was feeling particularly well and helped Rose and Amelia decorate the tree. Christmas Cards came by every post and Amy was overwhelmed to get one from Ned. Presents were exchanged and Mrs Gipps excelled herself with her Christmas menus. The only thing to mar the festivities so far as Amelia was concerned was the absence of Sophia who was spending Christmas with Grace and Gerald. John had received an invitation to stay with a Mr & Mrs Woollage. Amelia assumed they were business acquaintances.

On the day after Christmas, Amelia woke to find her room unusually light. When she opened the curtains she found that there had been a heavy snowfall in the night and it was still snowing. After breakfast she went into the kitchen to find that Ned had just arrived with an order.

"Can you spare Amy for half-an-hour, Mrs Gipps?" she asked.

"I think so, Miss Wallace."

"You come too, Ned" Amelia ordered.

Amy and Ned exchanged puzzled glances.

"Wrap up warm, Amy. We're going into the garden."

They obediently trooped out into the snow.

"Now" Amelia said as she bent down, made a snowball and threw it at Ned. It landed on his shoulder.

"A snowball fight!" Ned shouted, delightedly.

Upon hearing the screams and laughter coming from the garden the three ladies crowded to the window. Amelia, her face flushed and laughing, was being showered with snow by Amy and Ned. As Amelia began to retreat towards the kitchen door, a snowball flew past her and hit Amy.

"Come on, Amelia, don't give up! Together we can beat them!"

Turning, Amelia saw Mr Milton busily making snowballs. Obediently she returned to the attack. Amy and Ned now began to retreat.

"Mr Milton looks as if he is enjoying himself." Mrs Trevise said.

"Yes, I think he has helped Amelia a lot these last few months. But then he is a very good Priest." Rose agreed.

"Amelia looks almost pretty doesn't she?" Mrs Kitson said.

"I hope that, one day, Amelia will find the one meant for her." Mrs Trevise said, sentimentally.

CHAPTER NINE

January brought no relief from the severe weather with hard frosts, fog and bitter cold. One morning Amelia opened her curtains to find the windows covered in ice and the water in her ewer frozen solid. As she waited for Amy to bring her hot water she wished Aunt Isabella would agree to install a modern bathroom such as the one at No.13 with its cast iron bath and polished copper geyser delivering boiling hot water whenever required. Amy came into the bedroom carefully carrying a steaming jug of water.

"Cold 'aint it, Miss. Best wash only the bits that show or you'll be frozen." She advised.

Fires were lit in every room, and Amy grumbled as she toiled up the stairs with scuttles full of coal. Everyone became depressed and irritable. At the end of January Sophia persuaded John to book a box at the Savoy Theatre where Gilbert & Sullivan's "Ruddigore" was being performed and invited the Springfield Road ladies to join them. However, when the day came only Sophia, John, and Amelia ventured out. Mrs Kitson was not well enough and Rose did not want to leave her and Mrs Trevise did not like going out in the frost, particularly at night.

"I'm so afraid I'll fall and break a bone." She told Sophia.

Amelia thoroughly enjoyed herself. She was particularly taken with the heroine who was called "Rose Maybud" and couldn't wait to get home to tell Rose. John did not share Amelia's enthusiasm. He told Amelia in the interval that it was "rather light for my taste. I prefer *real* Opera."

Amelia was absorbed in the action on the stage when suddenly, one section of the audience began to hiss. The hissing became louder and louder as more and more members of the audience joined in. Soon people were standing up waving their programmes and shouting "BRING BACK THE MIKADO!" The noise was so great that Amelia could not hear the performers who struggled on. Losing patience, she sprang to her feet and shouted at the top of her lungs

"Do be quiet and stop being so rude!"

Eyes turned towards their box and missiles, previously thrown at the stage, were now thrown in her direction. When an orange landed on John's lap he got up, and, grasping Amelia by the arm shouted over the din

"We are leaving, now!" and dragging Amelia with him, led the way from the box.

"We shall miss the end." Amelia objected, breathlessly as she was hauled down the stairs.

"You have made an exhibition of yourself, Amelia. I am thoroughly ashamed of you, acting in such a manner. I hope none of our acquaintance were in the audience. You may have done incalculable harm not only to the family name but to the business."

"Go and get a Hackney, John. I want to go home." Sophia said taking Amelia's arm.

"Of course, Mama."

"Come, Amelia, we will collect our wraps."

Once they had collected their fur wraps from the cloakroom they descended the stairs to where John waited to escort them to the Hackney.

Once on their way home John was inclined to continue his lecture but Sophia stopped him saying

"I have rather a headache, John, and need to be quiet."

Amelia was relieved when they set her down at Springfield Road.

For several Sundays they had been unable to attend Morning Service. Amelia missed her talks with Mr Milton but, on the second Sunday after the trip to the theatre, and to Rose's obvious disapproval, she went to St. Mary's alone.

After Mr Milton had said goodbye to his small congregation he turned to where Amelia hovered ready for their usual talk.

"Don't get cold, Miss Wallace. Where are the rest of the ladies?"

"I came alone today. They find this weather very trying."

"Are you walking home?"

"Yes, it will keep me warm and it is not far."

"If you would like to wait in the Church while I remove my vestments I'll walk along with you, if I may?"

"Yes, I would like that."

For a few minutes they walked in silence. Amelia unsure what to talk about. She couldn't tell him about her theatre trip. As a Vicar he was sure not to approve.

"I saw you at the theatre, Amelia."

Amelia looked at him open-mouthed.

"You were in a box with a lady and gentleman. I was in the stalls."

"You went to the theatre? But I thought… "

"You thought that stuffy old Vicars did not go to the theatre I take it?"

Amelia blushed in confusion and was relieved when he laughed.

"My mother made my brother take us although he does not consider Gilbert and Sullivan to be real Opera."

"So that gentleman was your brother?"

"Yes, John."

"Did you enjoy it?"

"Yes, I did until people began being so noisy."

"Yes, I heard you telling them they were 'rude' I think you said?"

Amelia felt very uncomfortable.

"John said I had made an exhibition of myself. I suppose I did."

"I think you were very brave. Not many people would have done what you did. I admire that."

"Do you? John doesn't." Amelia said, disconsolately.

"John was only trying to protect you and your mother as a good son should."

"Yes, I suppose so. I missed the end. What happened?"

"I don't know. I left soon after yourself."

"Oh."

"Never mind, perhaps John will relent and take you to the Theatre again."

"I should like to go again but don't think John would take me. Do you go to the theatre very often, Mr Milton?"

"I'm very fond of Gilbert & Sullivan and go to as many productions as I can. Ah! – I see we have arrived at your gate so I will bid you good morning, Miss Wallace."

"Oh! so we have. Good morning Mr Milton. Thank you for seeing me home."

Mr Milton smiled, raised his hat and departed.

Amelia saw the curtains in the drawing room move as she walked up the path to the front door. Once she had been let in by Amy and divested herself of her layers of outdoor clothing she walked into the drawing room to find all three ladies apparently totally immersed in their several occupations.

Sitting down in an armchair by the fire, Amelia kicked off her shoes and held her feet out to the warmth.

"You'll get chilblains again." Rose warned.

Amelia obediently removed her feet from the heat.

Not taking her eyes from her embroidery Mrs Trevise enquired

"Not many people in Church as it is so cold, I expect?"

"Not many."

"Mr Milton well?"

"Yes, Aunt Isabella, Mr Milton is very well, in fact he saw me home."

"How kind of him. What did you talk about?"

"Nothing very important – I can't remember now."

"Never mind, it doesn't matter. Good, here is Amy at last to tell us that luncheon is ready."

During the next few weeks Amelia thought about her theatre trip many times. She was sure there was an idea for an automaton in there somewhere but couldn't quite grasp it.

The weather continued bleak all through February and into March when there was a heavy snowfall which confined them all to the house for several days.

"No snowball fights, Amelia?" Rose teased.

"I think snowball fights are rather childish, Rose."

Amelia replied, dismissively.

"You enjoyed the one you had at Christmas."

"That was Christmas – I'm older now."

"Of course you are. Almost middle-aged."

"Don't laugh at me, Rose. I'm trying to 'become a dignified woman' as John told me I should."

"Why not just be yourself?"

Amelia huffed in a very unladylike manner.

"I don't like myself."

"I don't think anyone is entirely satisfied with themselves."

"John is."

"Your brother is probably the exception. Why don't you begin a new design? What was that idea you were telling me about? Something about pictures coming to life?"

"I don't feel like designing. I can't think of anything. The picture idea is impossible."

Rose looked at her closely.

"Are you feeling quite well"

"Don't fuss, Rose. I just feel – restless, that's all."

"I expect it will pass. It's being cooped up indoors. You'll feel better once the Spring arrives."

"If it ever does."

After dinner Amelia wondered how she would endure the eternity that must pass before she could go to bed and lose herself in sleep. As she sat, idly pulling at a loose thread on her dress, she listened to Mrs Trevise and Mrs Kitson discussing the criminal cost of clothes.

"I was horrified to discover that I had spent £80 on dresses last year." Mrs Trevise was saying. "Fortunately, I am getting a good return on my investments."

"It is difficult when you are on your own without a man's guidance." Mrs Kitson agreed. "They are so good at that sort of thing. My employer, Mr. McInnes, taught me how to invest my money wisely for which I shall always be grateful."

The conversation then turned to the type of shares and the likely return. Amelia yawned. Amy came in and made up the fire.

"It is a great relief not to have to worry about money, is it not?" Mrs Trevise said.

"Yes, it is. I'm so glad that I will be able to leave Rose very well provided for."

Mrs Trevise tutted.

"There is no need to poke the fire quite so vigorously, Amy."

"No, Madam. Sorry, Madam."

"Leave it now, there's a good girl. We won't need you any more this evening."

"Very well, Madam. Thank you, Madam."

As Amy was leaving the room Amelia called her back.

"Where is Mrs Brett, Amy?"

"In the kitchen sorting the linen, Miss. It's washday tomorrer."

"Yes, of course, thank you, Amy. I think I shall go to bed now. Good night Aunt Isabella, Mrs Kitson."

"Good night" the ladies chorused. Amelia, looking back at them from the doorway saw the two old ladies with their heads together talking animatedly. As she lit her candle and mounted the stairs to her room she wished she had a friend in whom she could confide. The quarrel with Martha had cut her off from the only female friend of her own age that she had ever had. Now, for the first time, she felt lonely.

March ended in a blaze of sunshine as if to atone for all the bad weather. Amelia had been sure that, once the better weather arrived, she would feel like her old self. She did not.

The Queen's Golden Jubilee Celebrations were only a few months away and John had managed to secure seats in a building overlooking the Strand so that they could watch the procession to the Abbey for the Service of Thanksgiving. All the ladies were invited and were very excited. Endless discussions took place regarding suitable dresses for such an important occasion. Amelia was only mildly interested and barely paid attention when, on the way to the office, Bert pointed out the miles and miles of decorations going up as the City was transformed.

Sophia became alarmed at Amelia's lack of interest in anything and, as was her habit when worried, mentioned her concerns to John over breakfast.

John cleared his throat – always a sign that he was about to make an announcement. Sophia looked at him, expectantly.

"As a matter of fact, Mother, I have been considering inviting Amelia to come on a boat trip down the River with myself and – er – Mrs Woollage."

"Mrs Woollage, John?"

"The widowed daughter of a business acquaintance. You remember I spent Christmas Day with them."

"Oh, yes, of course."

Sophia's heart sank. She had not expected John to stay unmarried for ever but she had hoped she would have a few more years before he brought home another bride. She wondered what Mrs Woollage was like – she did hope she was not another Selina.

"She has no children and is living with her parents." John continued. "I believe her husband was in the Army."

Sophia grasped the nettle.

"Do you intend to marry her, John?"

"We are unofficially engaged, yes. I have spoken to her father who insists that we wait at least six months to announce our engagement. He is a very respected and successful business man, a pillar of his local Church. He would never allow Lucy, Mrs Woollage, to go on an unchaperoned outing. He is very protective of her. I rather gather he did not approve of her husband who left considerable debts I believe. I don't think he can object to our outing if I assure him that my sister is also to be of the party."

John did not feel it necessary to tell his mother that an alliance with Mr Burnett would materially assist him and the business. He needed the confidence of the City which, owing to his mounting debts, he was rapidly losing. Once he became Mr Burnett's son-in-law his standing and therefore his credit, would be solid and he was quite fond of Lucy.

"I'm sure Amelia would be pleased to accept your invitation. I'll mention it to her when I see her tomorrow."

Amelia refused the invitation. Why should she allow John to use her especially after his remarks at the Theatre.

"I do wish you would reconsider, Amelia. It is an opportunity to find out what this Mrs Woollage is like."

"Yes, I see that, Mama. We don't want John to marry another Selina, do we?"

"I didn't say that, Amelia but, yes, it would give us an idea what to expect."

"Very well, Mama, but if she is rude to me I shall come straight home!"

The day of the trip was very warm and Amelia decided to wear a navy and white dress topped off by a hard straw hat, complete with pink ribbon – one of the very latest fashions.

When John and Mrs Woollage arrived in a hackney cab to collect her, she was dismayed to see that Mrs Woollage was wearing an almost identical ensemble. Selina would have sulked and refused to go on the trip especially with Amelia. Had John warned her about her appearance? And if not, would Mrs Woollage be shocked? As Amelia settled herself in her seat, Mrs Woollage smiled

"How do you do, Miss Wallace. I think your brother is a very lucky man with two smart ladies to escort, don't you?"

Amelia relaxed and smiled back. Mrs Woollage seemed nice. She was not pretty but had a pleasant, friendly face, and a lovely smile. By the end of the day, after a trip down the river, stopping for a picnic lunch, and later the trip back in the boat now decked with lanterns, Amelia and Lucy were firm friends and John congratulated himself on his perspicacity.

As they set Amelia down at Springfield Road Lucy leaned from the cab and said

"Perhaps we can go shopping one day, Amelia?"

"Yes please. I should enjoy that."

"I'll write to you soon and suggest a date shall I?"

"I'm at the office all the week but I'm free on Saturday afternoons."

"Very well. Goodbye, Amelia."

"Goodbye Lucy – Goodbye John, and thank you for the nice day."

Lucy lost no time in making arrangements for the shopping trip. On the appointed Saturday afternoon she arrived at Springfield Road in a cab and they went straight to Oxford Street alighting at Marshal & Snelgrove's where Lucy asked the Floor Walker to direct them to the Ladies Fashions. Amelia was very impressed, she was sure she would never have had the courage to approach such a grand looking personage.

Upon arrival in Ladies Fashions, Amelia was shocked to see mannequins wearing dresses adorned with animals – bird's nests, and even spiders and fleas! Being Amelia she didn't bother to keep her opinion to herself.

"I think this is dreadful, Lucy. Those poor animals!"

A supercilious lady assistant overheard the remark.

Ignoring Amelia she addressed Lucy.

"I think you will find that this is the latest fashion, Madam. Perhaps you would care to try one of the dresses on? This one is very nice – the eggs in the nest set off the shoulder very nicely don't you think?"

"As a matter of fact I agree with my friend. Nothing would induce me to wear a dress decorated with dead animals. Come Amelia."

"I'm so glad you feel the same." Amelia said as they walked away.

Lucy stopped at a counter.

"Look at these fans, Amelia. Which one do you like?"

"The plain ivory one."

"I think I prefer the rose silk one."

They spent a happy half-hour choosing their fans and from there they progressed to muffs where Amelia inspected several before settling on a large white fur muff with a capacious pocket in the lining.

"I can keep my design book in the pocket and work on my designs when I'm going to and from the office in the winter."

"Will you show me your designs one day, Amelia?"

"If you would like to see them."

"What are you designing at the moment?"

"Nothing – I seem to have lost my inspiration."

"I'm sure it will return. I expect you need a rest, that's all. Now, shall we go on to Gamages?"

Once there Amelia bought a brown velvet dress which she was sure would be useful for the winter although she agonized over the price – £2 19s 6d! But it would last a long time although she knew Rose would take her to task for buying a dress when she could make her one for considerably less.

By the end of the afternoon they were weighed down with parcels and getting tired. Lucy proposed they finish the day with an ice at Gunters.

As Amelia sat, surrounded by her purchases, eating her ice, she realized she had not had such an enjoyable afternoon since she and Martha had quarrelled.

In the cab on the way to No. 13 and tea with Sophia and John, Lucy fell silent.

"Are you tired, Lucy?" Amelia asked, solicitously.

"No, not tired – nervous. I'm very nervous about meeting your Mama. Perhaps she won't like me?"

"I'm sure she will. You're nothing like Selina. She was..."

Lucy hastily put her hands over her ears.

"No, Amelia. You must not discuss Selina with me, it isn't proper."

"No, I suppose not. I'm sorry. But you mustn't be nervous of Mama. She can be quite sharp sometimes but not with you I'm sure."

"John says that he would like you to come and live with us after we are married."

"When are you going to marry John?"

"Not for some time. Papa will not hear of us announcing our engagement for at least six months. Will you live with us, Amelia? It would make me so happy."

"I have been living with Aunt Isabella a long time – long before Selina died and I am happy there. At least I was happy."

"Has something changed?"

"I don't know. I had a friend called Martha but we quarrelled and I miss talking to her. I should like somebody of my own age to talk to. I used to talk to Rose when I was young but she is old now – over 40!"

"I'm 36 Amelia. I hope you don't consider me too old to be your friend?"

"Of course not!"

"And perhaps you could make up your quarrel with Martha?"

"No, I don't think so."

Amelia told Lucy all about James' proposal and Martha's unkind remarks.

Lucy listened to the end.

"Oh, dear! I can quite understand why you are so upset. Why not put it all behind you and forget about it?"

"Yes, I think I can now I've told somebody."

When they arrived at No. 13 Lucy fell silent once more.

Elsie opened the door.

"Good afternoon Miss Wallace, Mrs Woollage. Mrs Wallace is in the drawing room."

As they entered the drawing room Sophia rose from her chair.

Before she could speak Lucy said

"I'm so pleased to meet you, Mrs Wallace. Amelia and I have had a wonderful time."

"So I see." Sophia said as Elsie deposited their shopping on the sofa.

"You may bring in the tea now, Elsie."

"Yes, Madam."

"Do sit down, Mrs Woollage."

"Thank you."

Silence fell. Amelia could see that neither her mother nor Lucy were willing to start the conversation. So, it was up to her. She cast about for something to say. Finally she said

"I've bought a dress, Mama. Would you like to see it?"

Sophia grasped the proffered life-line.

"Yes, I would, Amelia."

After they had all admired the brown velvet dress and discussed the merits of the white lace at the collar and cuffs against the disadvantage of having to remove the lace for washing and then sew it back on again, Amelia was pleased to see that Lucy was no longer nervous and Sophia seemed quite at ease with her prospective daughter-in-law.

Soon afterwards John came in for tea and they went through their afternoon all over again. After glancing at the clock John said it was time he took Lucy home.

"I'll come back and take you home, Amelia, so be ready." He ordered.

As Lucy kissed Amelia goodbye she whispered

"Thank you, Amelia."

After they had gone Amelia remarked.

"Isn't she nice, Mama. Nothing like Selina."

"Yes, she seems very nice. Time will tell" was all Sophia would say.

On the way back to Springfield Road John asked

"Do you like Lucy, Amelia?"

"Yes I do, very much."

"Do you think that, as you and Lucy get on so well you could come and live with us when we are married?"

Amelia was very tempted to agree but something held her back.

"Let's talk about it after you are married. Besides I can't leave Rose."

John knew that it was no good trying to persuade her when she had that look. He was sure that she would come round in time. He was determined to get her away from Douglass's so that she could design for him full-time and the first step was to get her back home and under his eye.

CHAPTER TEN

Excitement mounted all over the City as the day of the Queen's Golden Jubilee approached. Most people had never seen the Queen as she had remained out of the public eye since the death of Prince Albert and all were eager to secure a good vantage point. The weather had been extremely hot with not a drop of rain for six weeks and everyone prayed that the good weather would continue. The day of the Procession to the Abbey was hotter than ever and the flags, the red, white and blue bunting stretching from one side of the road to the other all along the route, hung limp in the still air.

John and his party were in their places well ahead of time. It was extremely hot and all the ladies plied their fans vigorously.

Eventually the cheers of the crowd alerted them to the approach of the head of the Procession. They all leaned forward as the mounted troops, in their bright uniforms, the gold of the horse harness glinting in the sun, came into view. The crowd cheered louder than ever, drowning the sound of the horse's hooves on the cobbles and the roll of drums. Amelia looked down on an open carriage pulled by four white horses. Alone inside the carriage a tiny figure wearing a plain black silk dress and a white cap, waved graciously to acknowledge the cheers of the crowd.

Behind the Queen's carriage came members of the Royal Family some in open carriages, others on horseback. Then more troops followed by a Naval contingent. As the last of the Procession passed by below them John snapped his fingers and a bewigged footman materialized bearing a tray of glasses.

John waited until they each had a glass then he stood and raised his glass saying

"The toast is 'The Queen!'"

"The Queen!" they echoed.

As she sipped her champagne Amelia was pleased to see Lucy and Sophia conversing quite at ease with each other.

John had also noticed.

"I think Lucy and Mama will get along very well. Don't you, Amelia?"

"Yes, I'm sure they will. Lucy is so nice. Not at all like..."

"That's enough Amelia." He sighed. "Sometimes I wonder whether you will ever grow up."

"I am quite happy as I am, thank you."

"Have you thought any more about coming to live with us?"

"It's a big step, John. I need time to consider."

"Well you have plenty of that. Lucy and I will not be getting married for a while."

Amelia felt that she was always having to make decisions. Did she want to live with John? She liked Lucy very much but she did not want to leave Rose. But then Rose was more and more taken up with her mother. Amelia sighed, it was very difficult. She put it out of her mind. Time enough to worry about it when John and Lucy were married.

★★★★★

Amy was ecstatic! She had seen the Queen! She was wearing her new green silk dress and she was with Ned who had, by expert use of his elbows, managed to get them to the front of the crowd. For some time after the Procession had passed they could not move in the crush but finally managed to extricate themselves.

"Yer look a real treat, Amy," Ned complimented her as they began the long walk back to Springfield Road.

"So do you. I didn't know you 'ad a posh suit!"

"It ain't mine. My Guvnor is an old clothes dealer. I nicked it from 'is cart."

Ned stopped by a vendor and bought two 1/2d. glasses of lemonade. Then he guided Amy to another stand where he bought two ld. cups of hot-eels. Amy was impressed. She had never been so pampered.

As she munched and drank she told Ned.

"Ever since Madam found me I've 'ad good luck. I'll always remember it. I thought something nice would 'appen 'cos the night before I wished on the new moon for good luck."

"Yer like it where yer are then? Good to yer are they?"

"Oh yes. Mrs Brett, the 'ousekeeper is very strict but she's teaching me all sorts of things."

"Like what?"

"'ow to speak posh so's I can announce people proper."

"Why do yer need to know that?"

"Oh, well" Amy lowered her voice "It turns out that Mrs Kitson – you know the poorly lady – is Mrs Brett's mother!" she paused, dramatically.

Ned was gratifyingly astonished.

"Never!"

"Yes, and what's more, she's got loads of money!"

"She ain't!"

"Nearly as much as" Amy cast about for a comparison "as Queen Victoria 'erself! So I expect they will be 'aving dinner parties and that."

Then she added wistfully

"I wish my mother would turn up with loads of money. If she did I would give you some, Ned."

"Would yer really – fanks."

"What would you do with it?"

"I'd leave 'ome, that's what. I 'ates my father."

"Wouldn't your mother miss you?"

"I 'aint got no mother. That woman he married 'ates me as much as I 'ate 'er!"

Amy tucked her arm companionably into his.

"Never mind, Ned. Tell you what, you come back with me and I'll find you something to eat."

"Won't yer missis kick up rough?"

"I shouldn't think so. Anyway they'll all be too busy telling each other what a good time they 'ad. Bet it wasn't 'alf as good as mine!"

In spite of Amy's assurances Ned was apprehensive and kept glancing at the kitchen door as he demolished the remains of a pork pie but as nobody came to disturb them he lingered longer than he had intended which was how Rose caught them off guard.

"Amy, I have been ringing the bell for five minutes. What are you doing here, Ned? Go home at once!"

"Yes, Missis. Sorry Missis." Ned beat a hasty retreat.

"Amy, I thought I told you when you first came that followers were not allowed in the kitchen?"

Amy hung her head.

"Yes, Mrs Brett. I'm very sorry."

"This must not happen again. Do you understand?"

"Yes, Mrs Brett."

"Very well. Now bring some tea to the drawing room please, quickly."

As Amy filled the kettle and placed it on the kitchen range she remembered her conversation with Ned. She must not do anything which could cause her to lose her place.

*****

At Ratcliff Court Ned was explaining to Anderson why he was late getting his beer.

"I saw the Queen 'erself. Little she is. I fawt she would be wearing 'er crown but she only 'ad 'er cap on. Amy said pr'aps she'd lost it."

"Is this the same Amy who scratched your face?"

"Yeh – but we've made it up."

"Evidently. So you are courting are you, Ned?"

Ned shuffled in embarrassment.

"Don't know abaht that. Anyway Amy don't get a great deal of time off. Worked off 'er feet she is. That Mrs Brett's mother is living with them nah. Makes a lot of work she does."

"Why is that?"

"Ill ain't she? Stays in bed a lot. Amy says she gets tired running up and down the stairs. I said to 'er if the old lady is as rich as Amy says she is and she looks after 'er 'till she snuffs it she might leave 'er somefink."

"How does Amy know this housekeeper's mother is rich?"

"She 'eard 'em talkin' abaht shares and that. Anybody with shares must be rich. Stands to reason."

"Yes, I suppose it does." Anderson said, thoughtfully.

Seeing him sink into a reverie Ned took himself off.

Anderson did not see him go. He was turning this latest piece of information over in his mind. This might call for a change of plan. He would have to think it out very carefully before he made his move. Nothing must go wrong.

*****

Amelia was surprised when, a few days after the Queen's Jubilee, Arthur came into the office unannounced. Usually he telephoned Mr. Higgins first. She sensed that something was wrong. Instead of speaking to Mr. Higgins and Amelia together Arthur told the Chief Clerk to wait in the outer office until he sent Miss Prentice for him.

"Is anything the matter, Arthur? Is Mrs Jarrett worse?"

Amelia asked as soon as the door had closed upon Mr. Higgins.

"I'm afraid I have bad news." Arthur paused, not sure how to go on.

"Yes?"

"The thing is, Amelia, I have got to sell the business."

"Sell the business!" Amelia was stunned.

"The Clinic have informed us that they have done all they can for Eleanor. They suggest we take her to Switzerland, where the leading expert in her condition has a Clinic. As you can imagine this is not going to be cheap and I need to sell the business in order to raise the funds. I'm sorry but I have no alternative. I must do all I can to find a cure for my poor Eleanor."

"Of course you must, Arthur."

"And I feel I must warn you, Amelia, that most business men would want to bring in their own designer."

"What you really mean, Arthur, is that no man would employ a female designer!"

"Well, since you put it that way, yes, I suppose that is what I mean."

"How soon will you want to sell?"

"As soon as possible. The Clinic is very popular, of course, and we have already booked a place for Eleanor. Patience is at home packing. There is a lot to do. I'm sorry, Amelia. I know how much you enjoy your work."

"How much money are you hoping to raise?"

"As much as I can get. The business is in a very good financial position and has full order books. I was thinking in the region of——" he mentioned a sum which made Amelia's head spin. She had thought for one wild moment that she could buy the business herself. She had some money saved but not nearly enough. She pulled herself together.

"Don't worry about me, Arthur. Just do what you have to do. I'm sure everything will work out for the best."

Arthur sighed, heavily.

"I certainly hope so. Best not to mention this to anyone until we have a buyer. I'll just have a word with Higgins and then I'll get back to Patience. I don't like to leave her too long."

After Arthur had left Amelia put aside her work. Would she still have refused James if Arthur's announcement had come before his proposal? No good speculating on what might have been. Her boats were now well and truly burnt.

She sat and brooded for some considerable time. Miss Prentice brought her a cup of tea and took it away again, untasted, several hours later. What Amelia needed was money. Where did business men get money? A Bank. She would go to the Bank and borrow some money. She had never had occasion to enter a Bank in her life. She remembered hearing Mr Higgins mention Hoare's Bank so decided that would be as good a Bank as any.

With Amelia to think was to act.

She rang for Guy, the office boy, and ordered him to find her a cab. Telling the cabby to take her to Hoare's Bank, Fleet Street she sat back, grasping her handbag tightly.

"'oare's Bank, Madam," the cabby announced.

Leaning out of the cab she saw an imposing edifice which reminded her of St. Paul's Cathedral. Paying off the cabby she made her way up the broad steps in front of the Bank to be met at the top by a magnificently uniformed doorman who seemed surprised to see her.

"Can I help you, Madam?"

Amelia cleared her throat.

"I wish to see somebody about money."

"Yes, Madam. Please follow me."

He held the door open for her and ushered her within.

Amelia looked round in awe at the opulent interior and the men walking briskly to and fro. Her escort led her to a grill behind which a superior-looking young man sat writing in a ledger.

"This lady wants to talk about money."

Her escort told him. Bowing to Amelia he turned and walked majestically back to his post outside the door.

The young man looked up. His look of studied boredom changed to one of startled amazement. He took in her plain clothes, her nervous manner and her misshapen face. This would liven up the day all right!

"I wish to see someone about borrowing money."

Amelia said, firmly.

"I see. You will need to see the Manager, Madam and I am afraid you cannot do that without an appointment."

"But it is urgent."

"I'm afraid the Manager will not see you without an appointment."

"I'll make an appointment."

"What name shall I say?"

"Miss Wallace."

He gave her a searching look.

"Just one moment."

He departed returning almost immediately with a small fussy-looking man who lifted a flap in the wooden counter saying.

"I am Mr Gilcrist, the Manager. If you would come this way, Miss Wallace."

Once seated in Mr Gilcrist's office Amelia refused the offer of tea and came straight to the point.

"I need to borrow a considerable sum of money. How soon would it be available?"

Mr Gilcrist blinked.

"I need some details first, Miss Wallace. How much did you have in mind?"

Amelia named the sum Arthur had quoted.

"That is a great deal of money. May I ask the purpose of the loan?"

"I wish to buy a business."

"I see. What are you prepared to put up as collateral?"

"Collateral?"

"The additional and separate security for repayment of the loan."

"What sort of security?"

"Do you own any property?"

"No."

"Pity. You must understand Miss Wallace, that I cannot lend you any money without security in case of default."

"But I would pay it all back."

"Also as a woman you cannot borrow money without a male guarantor. Do you have one? A relation, father, brother perhaps?"

"My brother, John Wallace, owns Wallace & Sons. Would he do?"

"Ah yes, John Wallace. Is there anyone else?"

"No."

"Then I'm afraid I cannot help you."

"Is it because I am a woman?"

Mr Gilcrist took off his spectacles and polished them with his pocket handkerchief, a gesture his staff would have recognized as covering extreme embarrassment.

"It does not help certainly but without collateral and no male guarantor, I'm afraid there is nothing I can do."

Amelia rose.

"I'll go to another Bank."

"You can try but I can assure you it would be to no avail – all Banks have to consider the risk involved and, I am sorry to tell you, Miss Wallace, that, from what you have told me, you are a very poor risk. I am sorry."

"Then I won't take up any more of your time. Good afternoon."

When Amelia got back to the Works she found Bert waiting for her outside and decided to go straight home. After he had spoken to her for the second time without a reply Bert left her to her thoughts. She could not raise the money that was clear. What were the alternatives? She could wait and see if the new owner would agree to employ a woman or she could resign and take up John's offer of a home and job. She would still be designing and perhaps John would not insist on her living with him. Then she saw the obvious solution – John could buy the business! That way she would stay where she was and John could eliminate a business rival which would be in his interests as the competition from the Continent was getting fierce.

She banged on the top of the cab. Bert's upsidedown face appeared in the aperture.

"Yes, Miss?"

"Take me to John Wallace & Son."

John was astonished when his Chief Clerk announced that Miss Wallace had arrived and wished to see him, urgently.

"Whatever are you doing here, Amelia? Is something amiss?"

"John, you must buy Douglass & Co."

"I beg your pardon. Have you taken leave of your senses?"

"Do listen, John. Arthur has to sell the business to raise money for Mrs Jarrett's treatment in Switzerland. I went to the Bank but they said I needed a male guarantor. I gave your name but…"

"Which Bank, Amelia?"

"Hoare's Bank in Fleet Street. I remembered Mr Higgins mentioning the name."

Leaning back in his chair John laughed, mirthlessly.

"Whatever is the matter, John. Shall I fetch someone?"

Amelia said, alarmed.

"No, no," he gasped. "Sit down Amelia. There is something I have to tell you. You had to know sooner or later."

"Yes, John, I'm listening."

"Amelia, I'm bankrupt."

"What do you mean?"

"I should have thought it was clear enough. I have no money. I'm in debt and can't repay the money I have borrowed from Hoare's Bank among others which is why they would not accept me as your guarantor."

"But I don't understand. Where has the money gone?"

"Gambling. I thought I could recoup. I should have known better. Papa warned me years ago. If only I had listened. Now I shall lose the business and the house and Lucy too. Her father would never let her marry a bankrupt."

"Can't anything be done?"

"Don't you think I haven't tried? I've sat here night after night going over the books trying to find a way out."

"Then there is nothing to be done?"

"No, next week I shall have to start putting the men off."

"Does Mama know?"

"No, not yet. She will have to know soon. We shall have to let the servants go and sell the house. Poor Mama, back where she started all those years ago and all my fault!"

Suddenly, to Amelia's consternation, he put his head down on his desk and began to sob.

Amelia sat in shock. Everything had fallen round her ears in the space of one day. But the worst thing was seeing her pompous, arrogant, self-centred brother break down. As she sat, not knowing what to do, she reflected that she had many times wished she could deflate John but not like this.

Should she fetch somebody? No, it would never do for John's employees to see him in this state. It was up to her to do something. Leaning forward she banged her fist on the desk.

"Stop this, at once!" she ordered.

John jumped and raised his head.

"Here, take my handkerchief. Mop your face, you look disgusting!"

Obediently he took the proffered cambric.

Amelia waited until he had wiped his face and looked more like himself.

"We must not give up, John. Papa would not."

"Papa wouldn't be in this mess. It's all my…"

Seeing that he was about to break down again Amelia said, sharply

"That's enough. What's done can't be undone. The most important thing is to act normally. Nobody must suspect that anything is wrong."

"No, of course not. Thank you, Amelia. I think I'm better now."

"Now, order some tea. It will be expected."

Rising from his chair, John walked to the door, opened it, cleared his throat, and ordered

"Fetch us some tea, Miss Newman, if you please."

Amelia waited until he had resumed his seat.

"We must not tell Mama until we have to. Will no one lend you the money? How much do you owe?"

"Its a large sum, Amelia. £10,000."

"£10,000!"

"I told you it was very serious. There is nobody I can go to. I've tried all the Banks. I did think of a money lenders... "

Amelia didn't know anything about money lenders but she didn't like the sound of it.

"Is there nothing you can sell?"

"I've sold all the pictures and Selina's jewellery. Even if I sell the house and Mama's jewellery it would only realize a fraction of the amount I need."

"I've some savings and you are quite welcome to that."

"I told you it was hopeless. It will have to be the money lenders."

"Don't do anything yet, John. Let me think about it. I might have an idea."

"Very well, Amelia. I won't do anything until you say."

A knock at the door heralded Miss Newman with the tea tray.

Once Amelia was satisfied that John was almost back to his usual self she rose to her feet.

"I have Bert waiting outside. I mustn't keep him waiting any longer, it is long past his time."

CHAPTER ELEVEN

As John helped her on with her cloak he said

"Thank you for your support today, Amelia. I don't know what I should have done if you had not been here."

"I'm sure there is a way out of this, John. We just have to find it, that's all."

"We don't have very long, Amelia. My creditors are becoming impatient."

"I'm sure I'll think of something. I'll come and see you here on Friday. In the meantime please don't say anything to Mama."

For the next few days she did nothing but turn possible solutions over in her mind, most of them totally impracticable. She had told John she was sure there was a solution and he was relying on her to show him the way but the truth was she could see none. One evening as she sat in the drawing room with an open book in her hand which might just as well have been written in Ancient Greek, Rose commented

"You haven't turned a page of that book for at least half an hour, Amelia."

Amelia looked up to see the three ladies regarding her steadily.

"I'm tired." She mumbled.

"What's wrong? Have you quarrelled with your brother again, dear?" Mrs Trevise asked.

"No, in fact…"

"In fact?"

"It's nothing really. It doesn't matter."

"When somebody becomes very quiet, hardly eats, sighs a great deal and looks as if she hasn't slept for days I think there is a great deal the matter." Mrs Kitson said.

"It's difficult."

"Perhaps if you tell us about it we can help?"

"No, there is nothing any of you can do. It's beyond anybody's help."

"Nothing is as bad as that. There's always hope."

Mrs Kitson sounded bracing. Amelia's patience snapped.

"It's all very well for you" Amelia burst out "sitting here all day with your sewing and your reading. You have no idea what the real world is like!"

Rose gasped

"Really, Amelia you…"

She stopped as Mrs Kitson put a restraining hand on her arm.

Amelia found now she had begun she could not stop. She told them about Arthur selling the business, the certainty that she would no longer be employed and therefore unable to design and John's huge debts. The only thing she omitted was John's breakdown. When she had finished there was silence for a moment then Mrs Kitson said.

"The ways of providence are truly remarkable."

They all looked at her, startled.

"For some time I have been trying to find something interesting and worthwhile in which to invest and here it is, right under my nose all the time!"

Amelia was not sure she understood.

"What do you mean, Mrs. Kitson?"

"If we are going to be colleagues you must call me Anna."

"Colleagues?"

Rose and Amelia looked at each other, puzzled.

Amelia decided that the shock of her news, coupled with her delicate health had unhinged Mrs Kitson's brain.

Mrs Trevise, however, looked delighted and asked, breathlessly.

"Oh Anna, what a good idea but do you think we can do it?"

"I don't see why not, Isabella. I have had a good training in the ways of business. During Mr McInnes' last long illness I ran the company single-handed although no-one realized it."

"Being women will be a drawback."

Mrs Trevise said, thoughtfully.

"It need not be, especially if we have a man as our representative in the business community. A man who will take our instructions. John sounds ideal. What do you think, Amelia?"

"I'm not quite sure I understand what you are proposing, Mrs Kitson."

"Anna, remember? I am proposing that I pay off John's debts and also buy Douglass & Co thus helping both you and John."

"But that would cost thousands of pounds!"

"Yes, I know. Thanks to Mr McInnes I have thousands sitting in the Bank doing nothing. Mr McInnes used to say 'make your money work – don't let it lie idle.' And there will still be plenty left over. Of course I won't touch the capital. I am sure I shall get a good return on my investment."

She laughed at their bemused faces.

"I want something to do. I'm getting very bored sitting here all day sewing and reading."

Amelia blushed.

"I'm sorry, I didn't mean to offend you."

"You didn't. You've given me an interest in life which is exactly what I need. I'm very grateful to you. Now, ladies, to business. There will, of course, be certain conditions."

"What sort of conditions?" Amelia asked, apprehensively.

"I'm only prepared to put my money into the venture if you remain as Chief Designer. Is that agreeable to you?"

"Perfectly."

"Good. Also I think we should all be on the Board of Directors."

"Women? Directors of a company? Is that allowed?" Rose sounded disapproving.

"I don't see why not and, so far as I know, there is no reason why we can't all be Directors. We will ask John to become our Managing

Director, that should satisfy the City. Now, Amelia, when did you say you are seeing John again?"

"Tomorrow."

"We shall all go and put our proposal to him, Is that agreeable?"

All the ladies nodded.

"Very well. Rose, get pen and paper, we must make lists."

They were very late to bed that night and Amy was kept up beyond her usual bed time supplying endless cups of tea as they discussed their plans.

"I've never seen 'em so lively." She told Mrs Gipps the next morning. "Now they've all gone out, at this time in the mornin'!"

"Gone out have they. Will they be in to dinner?" Mrs Gipps asked as she drew a chicken.

"I dunno, I expect so but they was very excited about it. Perhaps they're going to see the Queen!"

"Ever since you went to see that procession you've done nothing but talk about the Queen. Better peel some potatoes in case they decide to ask the Queen to dinner."

Amy sniffed. Mrs Gipps could make fun of her but she had enjoyed her day and, as she peeled potatoes, she re-lived every minute.

★★★★★

John was not very pleased when Miss Newman, trying not to sound surprised, announced

"Mrs Kitson, Mrs Trevise, Mrs Brett and Miss Wallace to see you, Mr Wallace."

Mrs Kitson walked forward – her hand outstretched.

"Good morning, Mr Wallace."

John automatically rose and took her hand. He could not imagine why Amelia had brought a gaggle of women with her.

Mrs Kitson waited until Miss Newman had set out chairs facing the desk and left the room. The ladies sat down. John settled himself behind his desk and waited.

Mrs Kitson came straight to the point and outlined her proposals, referring from time to time to her notes. When she had finished. They all looked at John.

John was not quite sure whether he was awake or not.

"You are proposing to settle my debts?"

"Exactly."

"Amelia had no right to tell you my private business. If you settle my debts I shall then owe you £10,000 instead of the Bank. I must tell you that I have no way of repaying you."

"There are conditions. No more gambling."

"Really, Amelia, have you no discretion?"

"Amelia has a great deal of discretion. It was not easy to find out what was worrying her. You should be grateful that she did tell us otherwise there would be no hope for you." Mrs Kitson said, severely. "As I was saying, there will be no more gambling. You will become the Managing Director of the Company answerable to us as the Board of Directors."

"A bunch of women! I shall be the laughing stock of the City!"

"Of course, if you prefer to become bankrupt there is no more to be said." Mrs Kitson rose and the others followed suit.

John flushed.

"I don't really have any choice, do I?" He said, ungraciously.

They returned to their seats.

"Once I am satisfied that you are not a liability I'll write off your debt."

John was silent for some time. Amelia wondered what he would decide as she watched expressions first of shock, then dismay and, finally, resignation, follow each other across his face. In a strangled voice he said.

"I accept your proposal."

"Good. I suggest that we instruct our Solicitors to draw up the necessary papers. We will then need to have a full Board Meeting. Shall we say this day fortnight at the same time?"

"Certainly."

Mrs Kitson pulled on her gloves, picked up her parasol and rose.

"Come, ladies. Mr Wallace has a great deal to do, we must not delay him."

As they left the room Amelia stole a glance at Mrs Kitson. She looked years younger, and was obviously enjoying herself.

That night Amelia found it very difficult to sleep. She had just realized the weight of the responsibility she was now expected to carry. She remembered what Arthur had said about her work not being up to standard. Would she be able to cope with the workload? She had no time to brood however as the next few weeks were very busy.

When the news broke it caused a mild sensation in the City. John settled his debt to the Bank with a flourish and was gratified to see Mr Gilcrist quickly suppress a look of surprise. There was great speculation in the City as to the source of John's sudden wealth. Some assumed that he had had a big win at the tables, others that a rich relation had died and left him a substantial legacy. None had the remotest suspicion of the truth.

John knew he would have to tell Sophia the whole story especially as Mrs Kitson and Mrs Trevise had made it clear they expected Sophia to be invited to join the Board of Directors. He put it off as long as he could but when Amelia got impatient and said that if he didn't tell their mother she would, he told Sophia the whole story in halting sentences, his eyes on the carpet.

Sophia sighed and said

"I am glad that you have told me as I have suspected for some time that you had started gambling again."

John looked up in surprise as she continued

"You see, I know the signs. Your father was the same."

"Father gambled! But he told me…"

"Yes, I know, he told me about it. He was hard on you because he knew the consequences of running up gambling debts. He nearly lost the business soon after we came here due to his gambling but he managed to extricate himself just in time. You must never go near the tables again, John, it could spell ruin for us all."

"I think I have learnt my lesson, Mama. Anyway with all those women watching my every move I won't have the opportunity, will I!"

Sophia smiled but said nothing.

Arthur was delighted by the news especially as Mrs Kitson had insisted on pushing through the sale as soon as possible.

On the day the sale was finalized Arthur called Mr. Higgins and Miss Prentice into his office and told them of the change. Mr. Higgins was speechless when he was told that the new owner was a woman.

"We shall be the laughing stock of the City." He exclaimed.

"Then we will not tell the City. This information is not to be mentioned outside this office. Is that clear, Miss Prentice?"

Miss Prentice astonished them both by leaping to her feet and breaking into the March of the Women.

"Shout, shout, up with your song! Cry with the wind,
for the dawn is breaking.
March, march, swing you along, Wide blows our banner—"

"Really, Miss Prentice, control yourself!" Mr. Higgins was scandalised.

"I never knew you were a Suffragette, Miss Prentice." Arthur said.

"I do beg your pardon Mr. Douglass. It is such wonderful news. This is just the start, soon we shall have the vote!"

"I think that will not be for some time yet. Perhaps in the meantime we can get back to the arrangements for the Heads of Department meeting."

"Yes, of course, Mr. Douglass."

Miss Prentice sat down and demurely poised pencil over pad.

For several days afterwards Mr Higgins was heard to mutter the words "viper" and "bosom" whenever he saw Miss Prentice, who merely smiled while she serenely carried out her duties.

Arthur called a meeting of the entire workforce and informed them of the merger of the two firms. Mr. Jarvis asked if this would lead to men being put off and Arthur hastened to reassure him that this would not happen. Mr. Jarvis did not seem convinced and sat down, muttering. Having dealt with that point Arthur went on to state that both firms would continue to trade as before under the new name of Wallace, Douglass & Co. He was relieved when it became clear that it was taken for granted that the new owner was Mr. Wallace. Not a great deal of work was accomplished for the rest of the day as the workforce discussed the implications of the new management and what it would mean for them.

Arthur was very touched when, later that month, he and Patience were invited to a farewell dinner given by all the employees of Douglass & Co. during which he was presented with a large framed photograph of the whole workforce posed in front of the factory. Miss Prentice presented Patience with an enormous bouquet of flowers and Mr Higgins, on behalf of the office staff, presented them both with an engraved silver bowl. Arthur made an emotional speech thanking them for all their loyalty over the years and wishing them well under the new management.

Afterwards, while Arthur and Patience were surrounded by wellwishers, Amelia found herself standing next to Mr. Higgins who was looking very glum.

"This is a sad day for me, Miss Wallace. I'm wondering if the time has come for me to retire."

"Do you want to retire, Mr Higgins?"

He shook his head, mournfully.

"The thought frightens me."

"Frightens you? Whatever is there to be frightened of? You'll be able to do what you want all day long!"

He shook his head.

"Oh, no I shan't, Miss Wallace. I live with my wife, three grown-up spinster daughters and the wife's widowed sister. They will all be telling me what to do. My life won't be worth living if I can't get away from them."

"The solution is easy Mr Higgins – don't retire!"

"A firm run by women! It's unheard of. It will never work. They will be taking money out of the firm to buy dresses and such like. And what do women know about the City? Nothing!"

"Please keep your voice down, Mr Higgins. So far as the City and everyone else is concerned my brother owns and runs the firm. And I can assure you that the Board has no intention of spending money on 'dresses and such like!'"

Mr Higgins shook his head in disbelief and Amelia was relieved when Arthur came over to speak to him. Soon afterwards the Chief Clerk left. Arthur watched him go then, turning to Amelia said

"I must go. Goodbye, Amelia. I'll try and get back to see you if I can."

"I do hope the Clinic cures Mrs Jarrett."

Arthur sighed and shook his head.

"To tell you the truth I don't expect very much. I'm only going along with it for Patience's sake. She won't rest until it is resolved one way or the other. Could you do something for me?"

"Yes, of course."

"Make sure that Higgins doesn't leave. He would be dead within a week if he had to put up with that gaggle of females all day."

"I'll do my best, Arthur. Now you must go, Mrs Douglass is looking this way."

★★★★★

At the first Board Meeting of the new company of Wallace, Douglass & Co. John took the Chair as Managing Director. Mrs Kitson and Mrs Trevise sat one side of the long table, Rose, Amelia and Sophia the other. Miss Newman sat at a small side table with her shorthand notepad. Various items of business were discussed very amicably. John had been sure that the women would have no idea of how a meeting was conducted and, when he saw that resolutions were being carried without too much debate he began to relax. Things might not be so bad after all.

Gathering his papers together, John said

"I think that concludes our business for today."

"I have something I want to say." Amelia spoke up for the first time.

"Yes, Amelia what is it?"

"I have found it extremely difficult this past year working for both you and Arthur."

"Of course you have, dear." Mrs Trevise agreed.

John shot her an irritated look. It was bad enough having women on the Board without having to listen to their inane chatter!

"What do you propose?"

"That we employ an apprentice designer. Someone that I can train myself."

"I think we would have problems finding a male apprentice who would be willing to be trained by a woman." John objected.

"What has my being a woman got to do with whether I can train a male apprentice?" Amelia indignantly enquired.

"It is not usual, in fact it has never been done." John told her.

"Then it's about time things changed." Mrs Kitson said, crisply. "And with all her added responsibilities Amelia should have a rise in salary."

John looked shocked.

Mrs Kitson continued, in a firm voice.

"I propose that we employ an apprentice, of either gender, and raise Amelia's salary a third in recognition of her extra responsibilities."

To John's chagrin the motion was carried.

Deciding to close the meeting before any more controversial issues arose, John said

"I now declare this meeting..."

"There is one more thing."

John sighed. "Yes, Amelia?"

"I further propose that we promote Mr Higgins to the Board as the Company's Accountant. I believe your Accountant is about to retire, John?

John wondered where Amelia got her information. He strongly suspected Miss Newman. It was a conspiracy of women! But, they would soon lose interest. Women could never concentrate on anything for very long. Mrs Kitson interrupted his thoughts.

"I think Mr. Higgins would be ideal for the post. Don't you agree with me, John?"

He opened his mouth to object but when he met Mrs Kitson's eye he closed it again recognizing he had met his match. This woman was enjoying herself. She would never lose interest. Better to make the best of it. He attempted a smile, not very successfully.

"Yes, yes, of course. I was just about to say the same thing."

"That's settled then. Perhaps Amelia could be instructed to ask Mr Higgins whom he could suggest to take his place as Chief Clerk?"

Amelia nodded.

"Is there anything else, Amelia?" John asked.

"No, thank you, John."

"Then I declare this meeting closed." John stated, firmly.

When Amelia got back to her office she sent for Mr Higgins.

"I have just come from a Meeting of the Board and I have some news for you, Mr Higgins."

"Yes, Miss Wallace?"

"You are no longer Chief Clerk."

Mr Higgins went pale and gulped.

"I quite understand, Miss Wallace, I have been expecting it. I shall, of course, work out my notice."

"We cannot allow you to leave, Mr Higgins. You are being promoted – to the Board of Directors as our Accountant!" Amelia grinned at him. "Congratulations!"

"ME!"

"Yes, Mr Higgins, *you*!

"We need someone to stop us spending the firm's money on 'dresses' I think you said!"

"I should never have said that, Miss Wallace. I don't know what came over me."

"That is all in the past now, Mr Higgins. As you have been promoted it leaves us without a Chief Clerk. Is there anyone you would like to recommend for the post?"

"Oh, yes, well. Excuse me, Miss Wallace, this has come as a great shock it was the last thing I expected."

"I'm sure it was and, as we are both on the Board, I think we can dispense with the formalities. As you know, I'm Amelia. What do I call you?"

"Horace, Miss – Amelia."

"Very well. Now, Horace, about this Chief Clerk."

"May I suggest Roy Green? He is a very hard worker and has made his way up from Office Boy."

"An excellent choice. I'm sure the Board will endorse your recommendation. But don't say anything to Roy until after the next Board Meeting."

Amelia was glad Horace had chosen Roy. She remembered all the help he had given her when she first came as a Typewriter all those years ago.

CHAPTER TWELVE

Inspector Burridge had been very busy with extra duties due to the Queen's Jubilee Celebrations but now he had more time to pursue a hunch and he descended once more into the basement of the Station House where the obsolete files were kept. After two hours he emerged, covered in cobwebs, and clutching a manilla folder which he took to his Superintendent who listened as he outlined his theory.

"It's a long shot, Burridge, but you could be right. You had better follow it up. Keep me informed of your progress."

"Yes, Sir."

"Good. Off you go then."

Once the door had closed on the Inspector the Superintendent chuckled and told himself

"A real chip off the old block that one!"

As a bachelor living in rented accommodation it was Inspector Burridge's custom to have Sunday dinner with his parents. His father was a retired Police Inspector and Mrs Burridge usually pushed them out into the garden so that they could "talk over all those nasty crimes" while she prepared the meal. Accordingly the Sunday after the foray into the basement of the Station House found the two men striding down the garden to inspect the cabbages.

After admiring their size and giving it as his opinion that his father would, once again, take first prize at the local Flower and Produce Show, Inspector Burridge broached what was on his mind.

"Do you remember a villain called Anderson?"

"Of course I do. Killed a warder. If I could see him swing I'd die a happy man. But he's probably abroad, out of reach and he's not likely to come back if he knows what's good for him. Could be dead of course. Why do you ask?"

"I think I've seen him."

"Here, in London? Are you sure?"

"Pretty sure. The Superintendent has given me permission to follow it up. I've found the file you wrote up. He went down originally for trying to steal some designs from a toy firm."

"That's right, Wallace & Sons. Mr Wallace was killed soon after in that big train smash. We could never get Anderson to say who he was stealing the designs for. I did have my suspicions when he killed the Chief Designer at Douglass & Co. after he escaped but of course I couldn't prove it. Anderson eh! What I wouldn't give to see *him* in the condemned cell!"

"I'm pretty certain it is Anderson. Can't be many men of that description with a crippled arm. It was the arm that jogged my memory after hearing you talking about the case. As I say, if it is him, I'll get him."

"You're a chip off the old block all right!" said his father, unconsciously echoing the Superintendent's sentiments.

★★★★★

Anderson sat in his room thinking over the information that Ned had given him. Anna sounded too ill to be much use to him and the last thing he wanted was a sickly woman on his hands. He was more interested in her money. The servant could be wrong about it being a large amount but there was no smoke without fire. Money would be just compensation for the damage she had done to him. How to get his hands on it? He could kidnap Anna and make her give him the money but he knew she could be stubborn and would be just as likely to die rather than give him what he wanted. No, there was a better way. A way that would enable him to kill two birds with one stone.

★★★★★

It was afternoon and Rose had settled down in the drawing room with her latest book from the Circulating Library. She had been lucky to get it, Rider Haggard's 'She' had only just been published. Mrs Kitson and Mrs Trevise were having their afternoon nap. Amelia was at work, Amy was busy in the kitchen so Rose knew she had at least an hour to herself. Sighing contentedly she opened the book and began to read.

In the kitchen, Amy was blackleading the stove. Mrs. Gipps had gone to the market after telling her

"By the time I come back I want that stove blackleaded until I can see my face in it."

As she worked she dreamt of the day when she was married and had servants of her own. My, would she make them work! She was roused from this pleasant daydream by a knock at the kitchen door.

When she opened it the man standing outside respectfully touched his cap.

"Excuse me, Miss. Would you have any old clothes?"

"Old clothes? No, I haven't."

He pushed past her into the room saying

"Perhaps your Missis has some old clothes she doesn't want any more? I can give you 6d a garment and no need to tell your mistress."

Sixpence! It was a fortune. There must be some old clothes with three women in the house.

"Wait here. I'll go and ask."

"Right you are, Miss."

Rose was deeply engrossed in her book and did not hear Amy's knock. Amy entered the room, coughed and said

"Excuse me, Mrs Brett."

Rose looked up, irritably.

"Yes, Amy. What is it?"

"There's a man in the kitchen 'oo says…"

"Hello, Rose. Not forgotten me I hope?"

"Anderson!" Rose gasped.

"'Ere! You can't just walk in!" Amy protested.

"Oh, but I have!"

As Amy stood, not knowing what to do, he produced a revolver which he held to her head.

"Now, Rose" he said, pleasantly. "All you have to do is come with me."

"And if I don't?"

"I will shoot this young lady."

"Oh! Miss!" Amy began to shake.

"It's all right, Amy. Leave her alone. I'll come with you, just don't hurt the girl. She's done you no harm."

Carefully avoiding sudden movements, Rose put her book face down on the arm of her chair and rose slowly to her feet.

"Where are we going?" she enquired.

"Back to the kitchen." He gave Amy a push. "You lead the way."

Once in the kitchen Anderson looked round the room and, seeing the open larder door, gave Amy a prod with the revolver

"Get inside."

Shaking, Amy walked inside the larder.

"Shut and latch the door." he ordered Rose threatening her with the revolver.

After Rose had done as she was ordered he kept her covered with the revolver saying

"Out through the kitchen door to the gate. There's a horse and cart outside with old clothes in it. Get in the cart and go down under the clothes."

Rose wondered if she had fallen asleep over her book but the revolver in her back and the hard stone of the path through her thin house shoes felt real enough.

The horse and cart were outside the garden gate; the man on the box had his face muffled in a scarf although the day was warm. She had hoped there would be people about but Anderson had chosen his time well. The road was a quiet one, this was the dead time of the afternoon, and the road was deserted. She climbed into the cart and down into the musty smelling clothes. Anderson piled more clothes on top of her until she thought she would suffocate. Then he gave the order to move, taking her she knew not where.

*****

Amy had shut herself in the pantry more than once and, as there was no latch on the inside had had to wait for some one to let her out. She knew that the ladies would not come downstairs for some time yet and Mrs Brett could be anywhere by then. She looked round the room in the hope that she would see something she could use to break down the door. It was a small room, one wall was covered with shelves on which were cold pies, jellies, a bread crock and under the shelves potatoes, carrots – nothing to help. The window! She ran to the back of the room and tried to reach the window but it was set too high in the wall and, even if she could reach it, she realized it was far too small for her to climb through. She looked round again – there might be something she had missed. On the wall opposite the shelves was a white marble cold slab with a bowl covered with muslin containing butter, also milk in a jug; she took a mouthful hoping it would give her inspiration. Her eyes rose to the ceiling from which hams, bacon and dried herbs hung on hooks. There was no way out. What was she to do? What was happening to Mrs Brett? She began to bang on the door as hard as she could – somebody must hear. As she did so she tried to remember whether she had said a taboo word during the morning.

Some time later Ned came through the open kitchen door.

"Amy" he called, no reply.

"Amy, where are yer?"

He heard a banging coming from the larder which he opened to be confronted by a dishevelled and wild-eyed Amy.

"Shut yerself in agin, did yer?" he laughed. To his amazement Amy burst into tears.

Ned was nonplussed. He tentatively put his arm round her. Amy sobbed louder than ever.

Mrs Kitson, coming into the kitchen at that moment saw what she thought was "carryings on."

"What have you been doing, Ned? We trusted you. I'm bitterly disappointed. What have you to say for yourself?"

"'Old on, Missis. I ain't done nuffink. I found 'er locked in the larder when I cum to deliver the meat."

He indicated the parcel on the kitchen table.

"How many times do we have to tell you never to let the door shut on you, Amy? You really are a stupid girl!"

Beyond speech, Amy sobbed louder than ever.

"Pull yourself together, girl."

"Oh! My Gawd!" Amy managed at last.

"Don't blaspheme. Sit down and compose yourself."

Amy sat down on a kitchen chair and dropped her head on the table, still mumbling.

"Speak up girl." Mrs Kitson said, impatiently.

Amy raised her tear-stained face.

"It's all my fault – I dropped a knife this morning!"

"What's all your fault?"

"Mrs Brett. She's bin took!"

"Took? What do you mean 'took?' she's in the drawing room, reading as well you know. Probably didn't hear you, although how anyone could fail to hear the noise you're making, I don't know."

Amy banged the table with her fist in frustration.

"She's bin took, I tell yer!"

"Let's find out, shall we?" Mrs Kitson led the way into the drawing room which was empty.

"What is happening?" Mrs Trevise asked as she entered the room. "There seems to be a great deal of noise."

"Amy seems to think that Rose has been 'taken'. I think it is a lot of nonsense."

"Look, her book. She would *never* leave a book like that, she is always most careful. Something *must* have happened to her."

"That's what I keep telling yer – *she's bin took!"*

"But by whom?"

"Some bloke."

Remembering Amy's perfect recall Mrs Kitson said

"Start at the beginning Amy."

"Well, I got up this morning…"

"Start where Mrs Gipps went out."

"Well Mrs Gipps says 'By the time I come back I want that stove blackleaded until I can see my face in it' then she goes and I goes into the pantry and gets out the blacklead and brush and starts blackleading the stove…"

They all listened with varying degrees of impatience until Amy got to the point in the narrative where Rose exclaimed "Anderson!" Mrs Kitson gave a cry and abruptly sat down on the sofa.

"Are you sure that's the name she said?" Mrs Trevise asked.

"Oh, yes, Madam, plain as anything."

"Very well, continue."

Amy described how she was taken at gunpoint to the kitchen and how Rose was made to shut her in the larder.

"What did this geezer look like?" Ned asked.

Amy described him in the minutest detail.

"That's 'im! I know 'im! It's our lodger!"

"Are you sure, Ned. Even if it is he, how would he know where to find Rose?" Mrs Kitson asked.

Ned smacked his head with his palm.

"It's all my fault, Missis. 'ow could I 'ave bin so stupid! I told 'im. I didn't mean no 'arm."

"Don't reproach yourself, Ned." Mrs Kitson told him, gently. "You were not to know. Have you any idea where he might have taken her, Amy? Think!"

Amy screwed up her face, twisted her apron in her hands and finally said

"'e didn't say but 'e said somethink before they went."

"What was it?"

"I couldn't 'ear very well but somethink about clothes."

"Clothes? You must have misheard."

"No, 'ang on!" Ned said, excitedly.

"Me old man is a old clothes salesman. 'E must be mixed up in this somewhere. They're always off down the Kettle Drum, drinkin."

Before they could pursue this line of enquiry Amelia arrived home and they all started talking at once. Amelia heard the name "Rose."

"Rose – has something happened to Rose, Anna?"

Mrs Kitson informed her of the events of the afternoon.

"Anderson! I hoped he was dead."

"I only wish he were" said Mrs Kitson, feelingly.

"We must get the Police."

Mrs Gipps knocked and entered.

"Excuse me, Madam. I found this letter addressed to Mrs Kitson under the meat and Amy seems to have run away – she's left the stove only half blackleaded."

"No, Mrs Gipps, Amy is here. She has had a very nasty shock. Would you take her to the kitchen and make her a cup of sweet tea."

Greatly wondering, Mrs Gipps took Amy out to the kitchen where Amy, recovering rapidly, sipped her tea and recounted, once again and in detail, the events of the afternoon to an astonished Mrs Gipps.

In the drawing room Mrs Kitson quickly tore open the envelope and began reading the letter. As she did so her lips set into a thin line. The others waited. Finally she folded the letter, replaced it in the envelope and looked round at the expectant faces.

"It's from Anderson. He demands £20,000 to be put into a bag and taken to St. George's-in-the-East Church tonight at 10 o'clock exactly or he will kill Rose."

"What else does it say?" Amelia asked.

"He wants it to be taken by…" she hesitated then looking at Amelia said

"He wants you to take it, Amelia."

"But he doesn't know my name – he can't. Simon never used it."

"You had better read the letter for yourself."

Mrs Kitson handed the envelope to her. Amelia extracted the letter and read aloud

"£20,000 – Church – 10 o'clock – to be brought by the ugly woman or I will kill your precious daughter. She is to go in to the Church where she will find more instructions on the first pew, left-hand side. You owe me, Anna, for crippling me all those years ago. I always collect my debts. There will be no Police or Rose is dead. Once I have the money I'll leave the country for ever. You'll never hear from me again.

Your loving husband

Albert Anderson."

There was a stunned silence broken by Ned, whom they had forgotten.

"Let me go, Miss. I'll smash 'is 'ead in for yer!"

"Thank you, Ned but I don't think that will do."

"I'll pay the money." Mrs Kitson said.

"Do you think that he will keep his word and let her go?"

"I don't trust him, Isabella but what else can we do?"

"We can go to the Police."

"But you saw what he said in the letter. No Police."

Amelia reminded them.

"We need a fresh mind on the subject and I think I know just the person." Mrs Trevise said.

"It must be somebody we can trust, Aunt."

"Ned, run round to St Mary's Vicarage and ask Mr Milton if he would be kind enough to come round. Tell him that it is urgent."

Pleased to have something positive to do, Ned sped off. They sat in silence until Ned returned with a worried looking Mr Milton.

"I ain't told 'im nuffink" Ned informed them.

"Is something wrong? It sounded serious."

"It is serious, Mr Milton." Mrs Trevise told him. "Please sit down. Ned, go and ask Mrs Gipps to bring in some tea. Perhaps you would like to explain our dilemma to Mr Milton, Anna."

Edmund listened, not interrupting. Mrs Kitson finished speaking.

"This is very disturbing, Mrs Kitson. I don't think Amelia should go, it is too dangerous. I'll go instead."

"No, no, that won't do." Amelia said, in her agitation putting her hand on his arm. "It must be *me. I* must rescue Rose."

"Of course Mrs Brett must be rescued but the Police have to be called."

Amy ran into the room. She was flushed and looked very excited.

"Inspector Burridge to see Mrs Brett, Madam."

They all turned towards the door.

"Blimey! The Peelers!" Ned exclaimed.

Inspector Burridge entered the room saying

"Good afternoon, ladies. I should like to speak to Mrs Brett on an important Police matter. Is she available?"

They looked at one another.

Edmund took charge.

"Mrs Brett is not here, Inspector. Can we be of any assistance?"

"I prefer to speak to Mrs Brett, Sir, if you don't mind."

"Can I have a word with you in private, Inspector?"

"Oh, no, Edmund, no – remember what he said – he'll kill her!" Amelia begged.

The Inspector gave her a searching look.

"Is this something to do with Anderson? If so you had better tell me. He's extremely dangerous."

Edmund took Amelia's hand and patted it.

"Yes, Inspector, we know. Mrs. Kitson, I think we had better show the Inspector the letter."

Without a word Mrs Kitson handed the letter over.

After he had perused it the Inspector said

"This is very grave."

"You can see what he says about the Police so you won't interfere will you?" Amelia pleaded tearfully.

"No choice, Miss. Don't worry. We're used to dealing with this sort of thing. He'll never know we're there I promise. Then, once you've handed over the money, we'll nab him."

"It's getting late. How can I get £20,000 from the Bank – it will be shut by now!" Mrs Kitson rung her hands.

"Leave that to me, Madam. I'll go back to the Station and make the arrangements. I shall come back at 9.30 with a cab and the money."

"I'm going in the cab with Amelia." Edmund insisted.

"Very well, Sir."

"Supposing he's watching the house? He will have seen you come in."

"That can't be helped. We'll just have to hope he isn't but to be on the safe side I'll tell you what we'll do."

A few minutes later Mrs Trevise opened the front door and ushered the Inspector out saying, loudly as she did so

"So sorry we could not help you, Inspector."

"That's quite all right, Madam. Good night."

Inspector Burridge proceeded on his way, whistling.

Inside the house Edmund was giving instructions.

"Now, Amelia, you and I will leave the house at 9.30 and hail the cab. Inspector Burridge will be inside with the money. Ned, you follow in another cab – here's a sovereign for the fare. I may need you. Mrs Trevise and Mrs Kitson I want you to stay here. Amy, you stay and look after the ladies."

"But I want to go with Ned." Amy objected.

"Do as the gentleman tells yer." Ned ordered.

"Yes, Ned. Here" she dug into her apron pocket "take this." She handed him what looked like a piece of dried-up leather.

Ned took it turning it over in his hands.

"What is it?"

"It's me good luck piece – it's dried calve's tongue. The man said it would guard you against assault. He said it never fails!"

Thinking it better not to remind her that it had not prevented her from being forcibly put into the larder, Ned only said

"Fanks" and slipped it into his pocket.

"Perhaps we could have some refreshment, Mrs Trevise. I think it is going to be a long night."

"Yes, of course. Amy go and see what you can find in the larder."

Amy went very pale and began to shake.

"Don't worry, I'll come wiv yer." Ned said and, taking her hand, led her from the room.

After they had eaten Edmund took out his pocket watch and said

"It's time you were getting ready, Amelia."

A few minutes later, Mrs Kitson and Mrs Trevise waved them goodbye. As they went back into the drawing room Mrs Kitson said

"All we can do now is wait and pray."

CHAPTER THIRTEEN

Inspector Burridge waited until they were seated opposite him then handed Amelia a large handbag.

"Is it all here?" Amelia asked.

"Yes, Miss. Better not open it though."

Settling himself comfortably Inspector Burridge folded his arms, leaned back and closed his eyes.

Amelia stole her hand into Edmund's who held it tight.

Sooner than she would have liked the cab stopped.

The Inspector opened his eyes and leaned forward.

"Here we are, Cable Street. Now Miss, once you get out of the cab turn down Cannon Street Road, that's the one opposite where we are now. Walk down the left-hand side and you'll come to the Church Gate."

Amelia reluctantly removed her hand from Edmund's.

"I don't want you to go, Amelia. I'll go." Edmund rose.

"Better not, Sir. Although you won't see the men, I can assure you the Church *is* surrounded. They will have Miss Wallace in view until she goes into the Church."

"Are there no men inside the Church?" Edmund asked.

"No, Sir, too dangerous. Don't forget he's armed."

"Of course I can't forget he's armed. It's all I'm thinking about." Edmund replied, savagely.

"Don't worry, Edmund. I know everything will be fine. I'll be back before you know it."

"That's the spirit, Miss. Good luck."

Amelia descended from the cab. It was getting dark. The street lamps had only just been lit and did not give much light. Clutching the handbag in one hand and gathering up her skirts with the other she crossed the road and began to walk down the filthy street. After a short distance she came to the open gates of the Church. She hesitated then, telling herself not to be so silly, walked through the churchyard to the Church door. It was ajar, she hesitated a moment then, taking a deep breath, entered. Inside it was dark except for a lighted lantern on a pew. She picked it up and saw the piece of paper which had been placed underneath. Holding the crumpled sheet up to the light she read:

GO TO THE VESTRY, THROUGH THE DOOR, WALK ROUND THE CHURCH TO STONE STEPS GO THROUGH THE DOOR AT THE BOTTOM OF THE STEPS. REMEMBER – NO POLICE.

Coming out of the vestry door she held the lantern high as she walked round the outside of the Church until she came to some stone steps leading to a wooden door. Pushing it open, she went through and found herself in the Church undercroft. It was dark and smelt of wet earth. She raised the lantern and looked round the room. It appeared to be a storeroom and was cluttered with old pews, blocks of stone and filth.

"Are you there?" she called.

No reply. She ventured further into the room, as she did so a shadowy figure loomed out of the darkness.

"Give me the lantern. I want to see you."

Reluctantly she handed over the lantern which was held up to her face.

"Good. We've met before, Miss Wallace. Simon told me all about you. Interfering little Miss as I remember. Can't say that time has improved your looks."

Amelia was determined not to let him see how frightened she was.

"Where is Rose? I'm not going to let you kill her like you killed Simon!"

"Who says I killed Simon?"

"I do. I heard you."

"Did you now. I've often wondered. To business. Give me the handbag and I'll take you to dear Rose."

Transferring the lantern to his left hand he picked up the handbag.

"Come this way."

He led her to the back of the crypt.

"She's here."

Amelia peered but could see nothing.

"Where? I can't see her."

"There!"

As he moved the lantern she saw a small, half-open wooden door set back in the thickness of the wall.

"She's quite safe. She's in there."

Amelia had to stoop to get through the low doorway. She could see nothing. She turned and held out her hand.

"Give me the lantern."

"You don't need the lantern. You and your precious Rose can rot together. Nobody will ever find you here!"

Before she realized what was happening he had pushed her violently through the doorway. She fell to the floor then with a crash the door slammed shut and she was in pitch darkness.

"Come back!"

Amelia tried to get up but was entangled in her skirts.

There was a scraping sound then silence.

Amelia crawled further into the room.

"Rose, Rose, where are you?"

There was no reply. She began to crawl forward, cutting her hands on the sharp pieces of stone that littered the floor. Suddenly she felt a foot, then cloth. It must be Rose but why didn't she answer? Was she dead? Amelia ran her hands up the body until she came to the face. The mouth was covered with a tight cloth which it look her some time to work loose.

"Amelia!" Rose gasped for air. "Can you untie my hands?"

Feeling for her shoulders and then down her arms, Amelia found Rose's hands were tied with what felt like a thick cord. It seemed hours before she made any headway with the tight knots but, finally, Rose was free.

Rose sighed with relief.

"Can you stand?" Amelia asked, anxiously

"Give me your hand and help me up. We must not lose each other. I have no idea how large this room is."

Once they were standing hand in hand Rose said

"We must find the door, but how?"

"If we find the wall we can follow it until we come to the door."

Holding hands and stretching the other out in front of them they began to move forward. After a few shuffling steps they came into contact with a stone wall.

"Move to the left." Amelia instructed.

After several paces they came to an angle.

"This must be a small room, Rose. Let's feel our way along this side."

In a very short time they had felt their way round three sides of the room finding not a trace of a door.

"It's hopeless, Amelia. We're going to die here. Nobody knows where we are."

"Yes, they do. We must not panic, Rose. Edmund and Ned are outside. Edmund will never let us die. We must not give up. Come on. If the door was not on the other walls it must be on this one."

They resumed their shuffling walk round the room. Suddenly Amelia's hand encountered wood instead of stone.

"I think we've found it, Rose. We'll soon be out."

She said, excitedly.

"Don't let go of my hand, Amelia."

Amelia began to push the door but it would not budge.

"It must be bolted on the outside. Perhaps we can find something that we can use to break it down. If we kneel down on the floor we can feel if there is anything."

Carefully they knelt down, still holding hand and began to make their way across the floor stretching out their unengaged hands as they went. They had hardly begun their search when they came up against the opposite wall having found nothing but sharp stones.

"It's no good, Amelia. There is nothing here." Rose sounded near to tears.

"We must not give up, Rose. Edmund will come and look for us once the Police have arrested Anderson."

"Is Amy safe?" Rose asked as they shuffled back to door.

"Quite safe, in fact she gave us quite a lot of information."

"I'm glad she's safe." Rose's teeth began to chatter. "It's so cold in here."

Amelia removed her cloak and wrapped Rose in it.

"Sit down here, by the door and I'll tell you everything that has happened."

They sat, holding hands, telling each other their adventures.

"Do you think Anderson will get away?" Rose asked.

"No, Inspector Burridge seemed determined to capture him."

"I know he's my stepfather but I hope he hangs."

"So do I!"

Amelia felt Rose shiver.

"Come on. We'll shout and bang on the door to let Edmund know where we are."

★★★★★

Anderson was elated. He had enough money to get him to the Continent and safety with plenty left over. He had avenged himself on Rose and eliminated the only witness to Jarrett's murder. He would go straight to the docks and find himself a ship. He had no intention of fulfilling his promise to the clothes dealer of paying him for his part in the abduction. He inspected the room. The door was completely hidden by the pews he had stacked against it. Nobody would even suspect that there was a door there. He had only found it by chance. Picking up the handbag he went up the steps. At the top he paused. He thought he saw something. Putting the handbag down, he took out his revolver and swung the lantern round. There seemed to be shapes rising from behind the tombstones. Anderson was not given to flights of fancy but he felt a moment of terror as more and more black shapes slowly rose. He fired at the nearest. The shape disappeared. He moved away from the top of the steps as the shapes resolved themselves into Policemen. He knew he had no chance of escape but was determined to make it as difficult as possible for them to capture him. As he prepared to fire his arm was held from behind and the revolver taken from him. He dropped the lantern and struggled but Inspector Burridge had him in too strong a grip.

"You're going to swing, Anderson." Inspector Burridge said as dozens of Policemen surrounded them.

The Inspector was just preparing to place handcuffs on his captive when Edmund, who had waited impatiently for Anderson to be captured, came running towards them closely followed by Ned.

"What have you done with Amelia? If you've hurt her..."

Anderson smiled.

"She's somewhere you'll never find her. Look on it as a favour – think what the children would've looked like!"

Before Inspector Burridge could stop him Edmund had punched Anderson in the face. Taken by surprise Anderson fell to the ground, hitting his head on a tombstone as he went.

Ned cheered

"Give it to 'im, Guv!"

"I didn't see that, Sir. Very careless of the prisoner to fall over. I shouldn't be surprised if he didn't fall over again before we're through with him!"

"Where is she?" Edmund hissed as the Inspector hauled Anderson to his feet.

Anderson wiped his hand over his face, looked at the blood and addressed Inspector Burridge.

"Will you let me go if I tell you?"

"Of course not." The Inspector replied and to emphasize the point snapped a pair of handcuffs on Anderson's wrists.

"In that case you can all go to the devil! I pay my debts. Hang me then and be damned to you!"

Try as he would Edmund could get no further word out of him.

"Come on, Sir," Ned said. "They've gotta be dahn there. Stands to reason. They're probably too scared to come up."

"Yes, of course you're right, Ned. I rather lost my temper for a moment. I'm sorry, Inspector."

"Think nothing of it, Sir. Quite understandable. I'm sure it's as the lad says. The young ladies are waiting until they know it's safe to come up. I can lend you a couple of men?"

Edmund hesitated then shook his head.

"No, thank you. I think you're probably right. They are too frightened to move. Too many people might make things worse."

"Very well, Sir. I'll leave the hansom here to take you back home. Come on you, move!"

Surrounded by Police, Anderson was led away to the waiting Black Maria.

As the men began to leave the churchyard one of the Constables handed Edmund his lantern saying

"You'll need this."

Edmund nodded his thanks and, closely followed by Ned, ran down the steps and into the undercroft.

"Amelia," he called.

There was no reply.

Edmund swung the lantern round. There was no sign of the two women.

"They must be here somewhere."

Edmund swung the lantern round again but could only see old pews, stacked against the walls and no sign of either Amelia or Rose.

★★★★★

Amelia suddenly realized that she had fallen asleep and from Rose's steady breathing knew she had also succumbed to the chill.

Amelia shook her.

"Rose, wake up! We have to shout again."

She knew that if they went to sleep they would die.

★★★★★

Edmund swung the lantern round yet again.

"Where are they?"

"Per'aps they went into the Church for sanctuary like." Ned suggested.

"Yes, of course, come on."

As soon as he entered the Church Edmund called.

"Amelia, it's me, Edmund. You're safe now."

They heard a faint groan.

"Did you hear that, Ned? Where is it coming from?"

"Over this way, Guv, there somefink 'ere. Bring the glim."

Edmund joined Ned where he stooped down behind the altar, and shone the lantern on a black bundle.

"Only one – which one?" Edmund said in anguish.

"It's niver – it's the Rev! 'e might know where they are. 'Elp me get this gag off 'im."

As Edmund removed the gag Joseph spluttered and demanded.

"Untie me at once!"

"Joseph, it's me, Edmund. What happened to you?"

"Anderson has gone mad. I was quietly praying in front of the altar as is my habit before retiring when he suddenly attacked me – for no reason! Of all the base ingratitude – you try your best to help these people but they have no sense of decency or…"

"Joseph, do you know where Amelia and Rose are?"

"Amelia and Rose? I have never heard of them."

He groaned and held his head.

"My head is falling in half. I must get to bed. Call the Doctor. Help me up."

"Joseph, listen carefully. Anderson has kidnapped two young ladies – I – I think he intended to kill them. The Police have him in custody…"

"Good – I shall prefer charges – it's…"

"Do stop thinking of yourself for once in your life!"

"Well, really!"

"They are here somewhere but Anderson refused to tell me where. They are in danger. If we don't find them soon they will probably die. Do you have any idea where they could be?"

"Let me think – if only my head didn't hurt so much. He seemed to spend a great deal of time here. I would see him coming and going at all hours of the day and night. I can't think where they can be."

"Ned, help Mr Hendry to the vicarage then come back here. I'm going to search the Church."

"Come on Guv. – lean on me."

As Ned helped the still groaning cleric from the Church Edmund resumed his search.

By the time Ned returned and reported that he had turned Mr Hendry over to his housekeeper, Edmund had completed his search.

"They are definitely not here, Ned. They must be somewhere in the undercroft. We will go back and remove everything in there if necessary until we find them."

"Right, Guv. Lets get on wiv it."

Once in the undercroft Edmund and Ned began to remove the old pews and pieces of stone placing them in an untidy heap in the middle of the room.

In a very short space of time they had cleared one wall with no sign of the two women.

"Come on, Ned, we must move faster. We don't have much time!"

Edmund said as he picked up a broken chair and threw it on the growing pile of rubbish.

Ned grasped his arm.

"'Old on, Guv. I fink I can 'ere somefink."

They both froze and heard faint shouts.

"There must be another room!"

"But where is it? There ain't nofink 'ere but wood." Ned objected.

"There it is again. I'm coming, Amelia."

"Rose! That's Edmund. Bang on the door." Amelia said, excitedly.

"I hear you" Edmund shouted. "It's over here Ned, help me move these pews."

Once they had uncovered the door it took only seconds for Edmund to unbolt it.

"Hold the lantern up, Ned."

As Edmund opened the door Amelia, who had been banging on the door with all her might, dazzled by the light, fell through the door and straight into Edmund's arms. Edmund held her as if he would never let her go.

"Cor, look at that, Mrs." grinned Ned as he helped Rose through the door.

"No need for you to stare, Ned" Rose said, sternly. Then, gently

"Excuse me, Mr Milton, but I think we need to get Amelia home."

For a moment Edmund looked at her as if he had never seen her before.

"Oh, yes, of course and you too, Rose, you're shivering. Come along Amelia."

"Has he been captured?" Amelia asked.

"Yes, he will never trouble you again."

Edmund helping Amelia and Ned following with Rose, they quickly left the Church and got into the waiting Hackney. Amelia, suddenly feeling very tired, leaned on Edmund's shoulder and closed her eyes. When they arrived at Springfield Road. Edmund gently roused her.

"We're here, Amelia. Come, my dear, let me help you out."

As they wearily walked up the path the door was flung open by an excited Amy.

"We see you from the winder. Are you all right, Ned?"

"Course I am. 'Ere, you should've seen the Rev. punch Anderson's lights aht!"

Amelia looked at Ned.

"That's enough, Ned." Edmund said, hastily.

Ned grinned and tapped the side of his nose.

"Silent as the grave, Guv!"

"Thank God you are both safe." Mrs Trevise said. "Amy, make some tea. Ned can help you."

"I told you my lucky piece would keep you safe." Amy told Ned as they made their way to the kitchen.

"'Ere, you can 'ave it back nah." He took it from his pocket.

"No, you keep it. I don't think I shall need it any more."

In the drawing room, Amelia and Rose were fussed over and made to tell their stories.

"He will hang won't he, Mr Milton?" Mrs Kitson asked.

"Yes he will, Mrs Kitson. I know he is your husband, Rose told me all about it, but he *is* a very evil man."

"I know. From the day we married he changed and I knew we had to get away from him. You will think me a very wicked woman, Mr Milton, but I'm glad he is going to die."

"Don't feel wicked, Mrs Kitson. At one point tonight I was on the verge of killing him myself. If he had hurt Amelia…"

"But he didn't, Edmund, and it's all over now."

Amelia said, gently.

Soon afterwards Edmund collected Ned and left.

Seeing that Rose was beginning to fall asleep, Mrs Trevise shoed them all off to bed. Amelia knew she would never sleep – her mind was too full of the day's events but, hardly had she got into bed than she was asleep dreaming of sailing down a wide river in a black and gold decorated barge.

The next day was a working one and she saw no reason not to carry on as usual. She did not mention her adventures to anyone in the office and had managed to put the whole thing out of her mind until Miss Prentice announced.

"Inspector Burridge to see you, Miss Wallace."

Amelia looked up, startled.

"Thank you, Miss Prentice. Won't you sit down, Inspector."

Once he was comfortably settled she asked

"Anderson hasn't escaped has he?"

"Oh no, Miss. He won't escape again, don't you worry. I just want to take a statement. I've already seen Mrs Brett. She told me you were here."

Prompted by the Inspector's questions Amelia forced herself to re-live the events of the previous night.

"Will I have to go to Court?"

"You may but don't worry. Just tell them what you've told me but it may not come to that. We have witnesses to the stabbing of the warder. He will hang for that. You didn't see Anderson stab Mr Jarrett did you?"

"No, but it had to be Anderson as he was the only one there."

"That is only what we call 'circumstantial evidence', Miss."

He rose.

"Thank you for the statement."

"Would you like a cup of tea, Inspector?"

"No, thank you, Miss. I'll be on my way."

After the Inspector had left Amelia tried to get back to work. She hoped she would not have to go to Court but if it was necessary to get Anderson convicted she would. She had hardly begun when Miss Prentice announced another visitor.

"Mr Milton to see you, Miss Wallace."

"How nice to see you, Edmund. Inspector Burridge has just left. I had to give him a statement. He says I may not have to go to Court."

"Yes, I saw him as I came in. How are you after your ordeal, Miss Wallace?"

"Quite well, thank you." Amelia was puzzled. Why was he being so formal?"

"And how is Mrs Brett?"

"She also seems to be well."

"Good."

Silence fell. Amelia felt she had to say something.

"Did you want to see me for any particular reason, Mr Milton?"

Since he was being formal she would be also.

"Only to make sure you had suffered no ill effects."

"Well, as you can see, I am in perfect health."

"Good. I'll leave you then, you must be busy."

"Yes, I am rather. Miss Prentice will see you out."

Amelia returned to her work. She heard the door close. She felt rather hurt. When he found her she had thought... Then she knew she had the answer. He had acted on an impulse and now wished he hadn't. She had hoped... She found that she could not see her design very clearly. She must move her desk nearer to the window, this bad light was affecting her eyes.

*****

Rose got up late. She ached from all the hours of lying on a stone floor. When she got downstairs she found her mother and Mrs Trevise in the sitting room.

"How are you, Rose?" Mrs Kitson asked.

"Rather stiff but I shall be better presently. Where is Amelia?"

"She insisted on going to her office. She feels she has a responsibility to the firm."

"I do hope she does not overtax herself. Women are not as strong as men." Mrs Trevise said.

"I don't think Amelia would agree with you, Isabella."

Mrs Kitson smiled.

"Yes, I suppose poor Amelia is different. She has to look to the future. She is never going to get married. Do you think she minds, Anna?"

"I'm sure she minds very much."

"Poor Amelia!" Mrs Trevise sighed.

"I don't agree with you." Rose said.

"I know how fond you are of Amelia, Rose, but we must face the facts."

"If you had seen..."

"Yes?"

"Nothing. I shouldn't have said anything."

"This wouldn't have anything to do with what Amy was telling me when she was lighting the fire this morning, would it?" her mother asked.

"How did Amy know? Of course, Ned."

"You were there, what did you see?"

"There's probably nothing in it, Mother. Mr Milton was comforting Amelia because she was frightened. Anyone would have done the same thing."

Mrs Trevise could stand it no longer.

"Would you *please* tell me what you are talking about? What happened between Amelia and Mr Milton?"

Reluctantly Rose told them what she had seen.

"I did wonder when Mr Milton was so concerned before they went to the Church." Mrs Trevise mused.

"But he is our Vicar and Amelia is one of his flock."

"We must stop this speculation at once. I don't like gossip." Mrs Trevise said, belatedly.

"You are quite right, Isabella."

"I must go and see Mrs Gipps about the dinner menus." Rose said.

"I have to write to my Solicitor." Mrs Kitson stated.

"There are some stockings I must darn." Mrs Trevise rose to her feet.

As they went about their various tasks each one paused from time to time and thought how wonderful it would be if…

CHAPTER FOURTEEN

Amelia had not been alone with Edmund since his visit to the office. After Church he was usually surrounded by people and only smiled and said

"Good morning, Miss Wallace."

She told herself, very firmly, that she did not mind. Fortunately she was very busy. They had made several attempts to find an apprentice designer but nobody suitable had come forward then, one day, Sophia made a casual remark as she sat having tea with them.

"I had a letter this morning from Grace. She said she found William doing some designs. She remembered how you used to sit designing, Amelia. William asked her to send them to you. She thinks they are probably no good but William was so insistent that in the end she gave in."

Reluctantly Amelia took the sheets which her mother held out to her. She and her elder sister Grace had never been very close. It was a long time since they had seen each other and she only remembered William as a rather rude little boy. She glanced at the designs and then studied them in some detail.

"These are good, Mama."

"Are they really good, Amelia?"

"They are excellent. In fact I wonder... Do you think Grace would allow William to come and design for us? Of course I would have to supervise him but he shows great promise."

Sophia thought for a moment.

"I'll write to Grace and Gerald immediately suggesting William comes to stay with me then you can discuss it with him."

Amelia was agreeably surprised when she met William. He had grown into a very handsome and polite young man. He was overjoyed when she told him she considered his designs to be excellent. She offered him an apprenticeship on the spot which he eagerly accepted. By the time William was established at No.13 and working with Amelia it was nearing the end of November and Anderson's trial.

To her relief she was not called to give evidence. When Rose asked her mother if she wanted to attend the trial Mrs Kitson declined saying

"I never want to see him again."

She did not object to following the trial in the newspapers however, where it was reported that Anderson had steadfastly refused to speak since the day of his arrest. He did not speak even when the Judge donned the black cap and pronounced the death sentence when, according to the newspaper report

> *"As the Judge pronounced the sentence the prisoner smiled as if he had just been acquitted."*

When Rose read this account to her mother Mrs Kitson said

"He is an evil man and deserves to hang but I'm glad it will not be a public execution as it used to be. Mr McInnes was taken by his father to a public hanging outside Newgate Prison. He told me that people were so eager to get as close to the scaffold as possible that some were trampled to death. He never forgot it."

On the evening before Anderson was due to be executed all the ladies were in the drawing room. Rose was reading Bleak House, Mrs Trevise was embroidering a cushion cover, Amelia was designing a singing monkey and Mrs Kitson was gazing into the fire. Usually they chatted from time to time or Rose would read them a chapter from her book but tonight they were silent, until Mrs Kitson said

"Tomorrow morning I shall go to St. Mary's and pray for the soul of Albert Anderson. Although he is a wicked man he is still my husband."

Rose looked up from her book.

"Would you like me to come with you, Mother, or would you prefer to go alone?"

"I should appreciate your company Rose, but only if you feel you can."

"Very well, I shall be ready." Rose resumed her reading and Mrs Kitson gazed into the fire once more.

The next morning, after a restless night, Amelia came down to breakfast to find Mrs Trevise alone.

"Anna and Rose have gone to the Church." Mrs Trevise said.

Neither of them felt like eating breakfast and from time to time each glanced surreptitiously at the clock on the mantelpiece. When the clock chimed eight they looked at each other. Mrs Trevise sighed

"It's all over."

Amelia nodded.

"Try to eat something, Amelia."

"I can't Aunt. I shall probably eat something later."

Soon afterwards Mrs Kitson and Rose returned. Mrs Kitson was very pale.

"Would you like some tea and something to eat, Anna?" Mrs Trevise asked.

"No, thank you, Isabella. I am feeling rather tired. I think I will lie down for a while. The last few weeks have been a great strain for all of us. Now the time has come to put it all behind us. I just want to forget that Albert Anderson ever existed."

"Very wise, Anna. Time to move on."

Rose and Amelia nodded in agreement. As soon as Mrs Kitson, accompanied by Rose, had left the room Mrs Trevise said

"Ring for Amy would you, Amelia. I want to speak to her."

Amy knocked and entered.

"Yes, Madam?"

"You know what today is don't you, Amy?"

"Oh, yes, Madam. That 'orrible Anderson is to be 'ung and a good job too. I said to Ned…"

"Never mind what you said to Ned. Now attend to me carefully, Amy. You are *never*, do you hear me? *Never* to mention his name again in this house on pain of instant dismissal. Do you understand?"

"Oh, Madam, I would never do anything to upset you. I like it 'ere. Please don't send me away!"

She began to cry, noisily.

"Stop that crying, Amy. Nobody is going to send you away, you silly girl. I just want you to promise me you will do as I ask. Will you promise?"

"Oh, yes, Madam. I promise. In any case it's unlucky to speak of the dead!"

"So it is, Amy. Very unlucky. Thank you, you may go."

"Thank you, Madam" and, sniffing loudly, Amy went.

Christmas 1887 approached amid the usual fogs, frosts and snowstorms. On Christmas Eve John and Lucy got married very quietly with only their immediate families present.

Lucy looked beautiful in a lilac dress trimmed with white fur and carrying a Prayer Book rather than a bouquet. After the ceremony the wedding guests repaired to Belvoir Road for the Wedding Breakfast. Amelia remembered the last Wedding Breakfast that had been held in the house when John and Selina got married. Sophia, seeing her smile, asked

"You like Lucy don't you, Amelia."

"Yes, Mama. I was thinking what a pity it was that John didn't meet Lucy first. It would have saved so much trouble."

Sophia became severe.

"It is not for us to question the ways of providence, Amelia."

"No, Mama, of course not."

"Don't let Lucy or John hear you express such sentiments. They would be most upset."

"I would never say anything to upset Lucy, Mama, she is my friend."

"I have to say, Amelia, that I bless the day John met Lucy. Ah, they are about to cut the cake."

Amelia watched John and Lucy as they cut their Wedding Cake and wondered what it felt like to be so happy.

Once the bride and groom had departed for a honeymoon in Italy, Sophia sent Amelia home saying she look tired.

Amelia threw herself into her work. She and William laboured for long hours over their designs. William had tentatively suggested that they target not only children but grown-ups and showed Amelia his designs – a mechanical monkey smoker, a bird charmer and a set of dessert plate, decanter, fruit dish and water jug all of which played different tunes when lifted from the table.

"I'm not sure, William. We are only known for children's toys."

"Exactly, Aunt Amelia. I am sure these will sell. Also I have an idea for a musical revolving cigar stand."

William told her, enthusiastically.

"Would people be willing to buy these grown-up toys?"

"We shall never know unless we try." William reasoned. "We have to move on, Aunt. The world is changing and we have to change with it."

"Very well, William. We will make a limited number and see how well they sell."

When, from the repeat orders it became clear that William's mechanical figures were a huge success, she suggested that he concentrate on these leaving her to design what she enjoyed the most – toys.

It was now well into the New Year of 1888. Amelia felt contented if not happy with her lot. She enjoyed her work, she had someone with whom she could discuss designs and nothing could be better, she told herself.

One Friday, after their usual monthly Board Meeting, John stopped her as she was leaving.

"Have you anything you would like to discuss with me, Amelia?"

"No, John, I don't think so. I'm very pleased with William's work and the Works seem to be running smoothly."

"I meant in your personal life. You are quite recovered from that Anderson business? I wish Mama and I had not been away."

"Yes, John, I have put it out of my mind and I wish everyone else would do the same. It was not your fault you were not here, I know you would have done all you could. As it was Mr Milton was a tower of strength to all of us."

"Yes, its Mr Milton I want to talk to you about."

"I have nothing to say on the subject of Mr Milton other than to be grateful he was with me that night."

"I see, Lucy and I did rather hope…"

"Yes?"

"Nothing. I have obviously misunderstood the situation."

Before Amelia was ready it was August and, this year, Mrs Trevise insisted that she go away with them to the rented house in Bournemouth. Amelia had no excuse not to go as William and Horace were quite capable of looking after things for a month. When she returned she felt much better, the sea air had given her an appetite and long walks over the cliffs had helped her to sleep better than she had in months. She had plenty of time to think while she was away and had made up her mind to speak to Edmund and find out why he was avoiding her.

On their first Sunday home they were nearly late for Church as Amelia kept them all waiting while she changed her dress for the third time that morning as Rose rather irritably pointed out.

Amelia found it difficult to concentrate on the Service which seemed to go on for ever but the final Blessing came at last.

As Edmund stood at the Church door saying goodbye to his parishioners, Amelia hung back, making sure that she was the last. Eventually everyone had gone.

"Good morning, Miss Wallace."

"My name is Amelia, Edmund or have you forgotten?"

"No, I have not forgotten. I prefer to call you Miss Wallace."

"Why?" Amelia asked, direct as always.

"Until I know whether… This is very difficult. May I come and see you this afternoon? I should like to talk to you."

"Certainly. What do you want to talk about?"

"I would rather tell you this afternoon."

As Amelia joined the others she wondered what Edmund could possibly want to talk to her about. Perhaps it was something to do with Anderson but what she could not imagine. She waited with some impatience for his visit. Several times she checked the drawing room clock, sure that it had stopped. Mrs Trevise and Mrs Kitson retired for their afternoon naps. Rose settled down with her book and still he did not come. Just when she thought she would go mad, faint, or both, Amy announced

"Mr Milton is at the front door to see you, Miss Wallace."

"Well, ask him in, Amy." Amelia said, impatiently.

"'e says 'e will see you in the garden, Miss." Amy said, obviously feeling aggrieved by Amelia's tone.

Rose looked up from her book.

"I wonder what he wants?"

"I have no idea, Rose. I shall go and find out."

It was a lovely, warm September day. Amelia found Edmund pacing up and down the lawn.

"You wanted to see me, Edmund?"

"Yes, Miss Wallace. Shall we sit down?"

He led her to a garden seat. Edmund twiddled with his watch chain, took out his watch, opened it, looked at it, snapped it shut and returned it to his waistcoat pocket.

Amelia felt irritated.

"You are in a hurry, Edmund?"

"What? Oh no, no hurry. I've something important to ask you, Amelia."

Amelia suddenly found that her stays were too tight. She could hardly breathe.

"Yes?" she asked, faintly.

Edmund addressed a rose in the flower bed in front of him.

"I have something to tell you."

"Yes?"

"I am an orphan and was found in a Church Porch by the Priest when I was a few days old. Having no family of his own he adopted me and made sure I had a good education after which I went into the Church – out of gratitude I suppose." Edmund fell into a reverie.

Amelia waited.

Coming back to the present, Edmund continued

"He was a very distant man and never discussed his personal affairs with me. He belonged to a minor branch of a wealthy family. There had been some sort of quarrel many years before and the family split up and lost contact. He was the last of the line and he inherited the estate just before his death. It was a complete surprise to me to find that I was his sole beneficiary. I own an estate in Herefordshire which I have not yet had time to visit. It is run by an Estate Manager."

"Herefordshire – that's a long way away."

Amelia felt dismay.

"Yes. My Bishop offered me this Parish but I know now that I am not really cut out to be a Parish Priest. What I would like to do is to open a boarding school for poor boys. Somewhere where they could grow and develop into useful members of Society instead of turning to crime. Boys like Ned for example. The estate is ideal as there is a large house and acres of grounds together with farms and cottages."

"That is a very good idea Edmund. I hope it goes well. We shall all miss you, of course."

Edmund turned and looked at her.

"Amelia – I have spoken to John and he has given his consent. I want you to come with me and help me to run the school."

"And John agreed to this?"

"He was delighted. He said…"

Amelia interrupted.

"I don't want to know what John said. How dare John, yes, and you, think you can run my life for me! This is 1888 not 1800. I thought you at least understood. I am very happy doing my designs. I had to fight hard to get where I am and I will not give it all up just to become your assistant away from everyone I know. I am happy here with Mrs Trevise and Rose. If I go to Herefordshire I shall be stared at and pitied and it will be 'poor Amelia, look at her face, she will never get married'. No, I will stay here where I am safe."

She jumped up and began to walk back to the house. She felt upset. She had thought when they were rescued that – he had seemed so – how foolish of her to think—

Edmund too jumped up. He went very white and, unconsciously echoing her thoughts shouted at her rapidly retreating back

"Why are you so *foolish*, Amelia? Why can't you understand that I am asking you to marry me – I love you!"

As Amelia turned and ran back to him Amy come out of the kitchen door to shake her duster. She paused, transfixed, duster in hand then, flinging the duster down she ran into the house and to the drawing room where she dragged a startled Rose to the window saying

"Come 'ere! Quick!"

Open mouthed they looked on as Edmund took Amelia into his arms and kissed her – several times.

"Oo'er!" Amy breathed.

"We should not be spying on them, Amy."

"But just fancy – Miss Wallace and Mr Milton. 'oo would 'ave thought it!"

"Go and get on with your work, Amy. Mrs Trevise and Mrs Kitson will be down soon and I want the dining room thoroughly dusted by then."

Amy rushed off to the kitchen to apprise Mrs Gipps that

"'corse I saw it coming. Been mooning after 'er for months 'e 'as. Ned said 'e was a cuddlin' of 'er something fierce after they rescued them. 'E is a nice gentleman. 'E'll look after 'er."

"Let's hope so." Mrs Gipps sighed. "My youngest took up with an omnibus conductor. Knocked her about. She left him in the end."

"Go on!" Amy said, wide-eyed.

"I haven't got time to gossip and neither have you. You'd better go and finish that dusting or Mrs Brett will be after you again."

Grumbling, Amy went to find her duster just as Amelia and Edmund came back into the house.

"Good afternoon, Miss Paget. Lovely day isn't it?"

Edmund beamed. Startled, Amy stammered

"Yes, Sir. Thank you, Sir" and fled, giggling, to the dining room where she dusted vigorously to the great danger of the ornaments.

Hearing his voice, Rose swiftly resumed her seat and picked up her book.

"Rose – do stop reading I have something wonderful to tell you!"

Amelia said as she entered the room. Rose looked up and smiled at her flushed face.

"Have you, Amelia?"

"Mr Milton – Edmund – has asked me to marry him and I said yes!"

Getting up Rose went to her and kissed her.

"I'm so pleased, Amelia. Congratulations, Mr Milton."

"Edmund has an enormous estate…"

"Hardly enormous, Amelia – large perhaps."

"Well, anyway there is a big house and he is going to open a boarding school for poor boys and I'm going to help him. He says that I can still do my designs."

"Where is this Estate, Mr Milton?"

"In Herefordshire."

"That's a long way away." Rose said.

"But you'll be coming with me, won't you, Rose?"

"I don't know. I can't give an answer now. I must have time to think."

"Of course you must. We must not rush Rose, Amelia."

"No, Edmund, of course not."

When the two elderly ladies came downstairs they were surprised to find Edmund ensconced in the drawing room. Explanations were given during which Amy brought in the tea. Edmund, suddenly realizing that it was nearly time for the Evening Service, rushed off and, over the teacups, the ladies got down to discussing important matters.

"When is the wedding to be, Amelia?"

"We haven't decided on a date yet. Not for a while. Edmund has to go and see what condition the house is in and so on."

"Then we have plenty of time to think about the Wedding dress and the bridesmaids. But Sophia should be here. We must not make any decisions without your mother, Amelia. It would not be right."

Mrs Trevise stated.

"We will invite Sophia, John and Lucy to tea, and Edmund of course, as soon as possible. Shall we say tomorrow afternoon? I'm sure William can manage without you."

Amelia could see that, in her mind, Aunt Isabella was busily organizing everything. She only hoped Mama would not object. She didn't want her lovely day spoiled by quarrels between the ladies.

In the office next day and after a restless night, Amelia found she kept drawing bridal dresses all over her sketch pad. She told William she had to leave early as she had some important business at home.

"This important business would not begin with an "M" would it, Aunt? Uncle John and Grandmother talked of nothing else at breakfast. Uncle John told Grandmother that Mr Milton – I suppose I shall have to call him Uncle Edmund – had asked him for your hand in marriage. Of course, they didn't know what your answer was but, from the fact that you can't stop smiling to yourself, I take it that it was 'No'! "

"You are quite wrong, William. Tell me, what did they say? Don't tell me if you would rather not." She added hastily.

"Well – Uncle John said Mr Milton had been to see him and he had been delighted to give his consent to his asking you to marry him. Then he said that – um…"

"Yes?"

"He said that he hoped you would see sense and accept. Then he said a lot other things I can't remember."

"I understand, William. I can just imagine what John said. What did Mama say?"

"Grandmother said how happy it would make her to see you settled."

"Thank you, William. They are coming to tea this afternoon. I wish you could come."

"No, I must stay here, besides it will be pretty boring I expect."

"But not to me, William. One day when you get engaged to a nice young lady you will understand."

"I dare say you are right."

That afternoon Mrs Gipps excelled herself. The cucumber sandwiches cut to such thinness that they were nearly transparent, slices of almond, chocolate, layer and fruit cake were set out on the best china and Amy, in a clean cap and apron, expertly handed round plates and cups.

John took his favourite stance in front of the fire and expounded on the joys of marriage until Lucy gently informed him that she thought he should sit down and enjoy his cake. Sophia could not stop hugging Amelia. Edmund looked pleased with himself and Amelia tried to stop looking at him all the time. Mrs Kitson was rather quiet and, when Amelia was telling everyone how she was going to help run the school and how Rose was going to help her, she became quieter still. Glancing at her mother, Rose reminded Amelia that she had not given her answer yet.

"But" said Amelia "I am sure that you will come. You have always been with me, Rose."

"We will see" was all that Rose would say.

Sensing that Rose wanted the subject dropped Mrs Trevise said

"Have you seen the estate yet, Mr Milton?"

Edmund replied that he had not but he had a description from his Estate Manager.

He was urged to give them full details which he did until Amy announced dinner. The evening passed pleasantly in plans for the Wedding.

That evening as Rose brushed Amelia's long fair hair Amelia sighed contentedly

"Isn't life wonderful, Rose?"

"I'm glad you have found somebody who loves you for yourself, Amelia, and it is plain that he does."

"Yes, I was afraid he only wanted to marry me to get a housekeeper for his school. This happened once before, as you know. Then there was James who *did* love me but I didn't love him. I nearly married him you know, Rose, but something held me back. I don't know what but I'm glad it did. Edmund said he was afraid I would reject him as too old, and I was afraid he would think me too ugly. I'm *so* happy!"

"And so am I, Amelia, you deserve to be happy."

Amelia swung round, taking the brush from Rose's hand and putting it down on the dressing table she took both Rose's hands in hers as she said, earnestly

"Please say you will come and live with us, Rose. It is a big house – you could have your own apartments."

Rose gazed into Amelia's flushed face. She badly wanted to agree but knew she could not.

"You don't really need me now, Amelia. You know you don't" as Amelia began to protest. "I must consider my mother, she is not strong and it has taken us so long to find each other again."

"But she looks so well now and she could come and visit as often as she liked."

"I am afraid it's not that simple. She is a very sick woman. Yes, I know she seems well at the moment but that is because the disease is in remission. She has consumption, Amelia."

"Oh, Rose, I'm so sorry. Then of course you must stay with her until…"

"I knew you would understand. But, I will come to you when you are due to have your first confinement. I was there when you were born and I intend to be there when your child is born. That will make it full circle, won't it!"

And taking up the brush Rose resumed her careful brushing.

CHAPTER FIFTEEN

Rose found it difficult to get to sleep after her conversation with Amelia. It would be a great wrench leaving her after all these years but she knew she had made the right decision. There was also Mrs Trevise to consider, she needed a Housekeeper.

She turned over, restlessly. Perhaps a drink of water would calm her nerves. She got out of bed lit her candle, wrapped herself in her shawl, slipped into her slippers, picked up the candlestick and quietly went downstairs to the kitchen where she used the candle to light the oil lamp on the dresser. As she took down a glass from the dresser and turned towards the sink to get her water she thought she heard some one snoring. Standing still she listened intently. Again she heard the snoring. Where was it coming from? She traced the noise to the kitchen table. Picking up the lamp she bent down and looked underneath.

"Ned! What on earth are you doing, sleeping under our kitchen table?"

Ned woke with a start.

"Stop shinin' that light in me eyes and I'll tell yer" he replied.

Rose replaced the lamp on the dresser as Ned climbed out of his makeshift bed.

"Well, Ned. I'm waiting."

"I've left 'ome, that's what."

"Why?"

"When the Peelers cum and took me old man away and I found aht 'e 'ad 'elped Anderson take yer I was that angry I just walked aht. And" he added, defiantly "I 'ain't going back."

"How did you end up here?"

"I lost me place with the Butcher. 'E said 'e didn't want no truck with villains as it were bad for business. I told 'im it weren't nuffink to do with me but 'e wouldn't listen, would 'e? Right nasty he was. I 'ad no money and nowhere to go so I cum to tell Amy I would 'ave to go away for a bit. She said I could sleep 'ere but I 'ad to keep quiet.

I didn't know nuffink abaht people creeping round at night when they didn't 'ave no business to." He added, truculently.

"It was your snoring that alerted me to your presence, Ned."

"I suppose yer want me to go?"

"No, Ned, I don't. You see I know what it is like living in Ratcliff Court. I lived there once myself."

"You did? Garn – you're 'aving me on!"

"Anderson took us to live there after he and my mother married. It is a dreadful place. However, you can't sleep under a table for ever."

"I'm going to get a job, Missis. A decent one this time. I want to get on, I do."

"That's very good to hear, Ned, and I am sure you will. Go back to sleep now and we'll talk again in the morning."

Ned yawned.

"Good night, Missis."

"Good night, Ned."

Ned returned to his bed and Rose got her glass of water. Really, you never knew what was going to happen next, she thought as she quietly returned to her room.

Next morning Rose entered the kitchen to find Amy giving Ned his breakfast. Ned waved his knife at her.

"Morning, Missis. I told Amy abaht last night" he said, through a mouthful of scrambled egg.

Amy looked apprehensive clearly expecting the worst.

"Are you going out looking for employment today, Ned?" Rose asked.

"Yeah."

"What sort of work are you looking for?"

"Anyfink so long as nobody don't expect me to do nuffink shady."

"Come back here tonight. I might have some news for you."

"All right, Missis. Fanks."

At breakfast Rose announced she had an urgent errand to run, then she walked round to the Rectory. When Edmund returned from taking early Communion and he was told by his housekeeper, Mrs Dimlow, that Mrs Brett was waiting in his study he immediately became anxious.

"Has something happened to Amelia?" he asked as he entered the room.

"No, Amelia is fine. I've come about Ned."

"Ned?"

Rose briefly outlined Ned's predicament.

"And I wondered whether you could help him find some employment. He is very willing and honest."

"Also dependable as I found. I think I can offer him something on my estate. How do you think he would feel about living in the country?"

"I don't know. I don't think he has ever been outside London but he strikes me as the sort of boy who would relish a challenge."

"Yes, I think you're right. I'll come round this evening and have a word with him. Will he be there?"

"He's still sleeping in our kitchen but we can't let him do that much longer."

"That is not very satisfactory."

Edmund rang the bell. When his housekeeper appeared he said

"Mrs Dimlow, please prepare one of the spare rooms for a young man I shall be bringing back with me. He will also be having dinner here this evening."

"Yes, Sir."

Another one of Mr Milton's stray dogs I suppose, Mrs Dimlow thought as she mentally reviewed the clean linen position.

When she had left the room Rose said

"Thank you, Mr Milton."

"Until this evening then."

Ned and Amy had been speculating as to what Mrs Brett's news could be and were surprised when Mr Milton appeared in the kitchen, took a chair by the table and told them both to sit down.

"Now, Ned. I understand that you are looking for work?"

"Yes, Guv."

"How would you like to come and work with me in Herefordshire? I could do with a strong lad like you."

"I should like that, Guv. Only…"

"Only?"

"I would 'ave to leave Amy, wouldn't I? I'm not bovered abaht meself yer understand but Amy needs somebody to take care of 'er like."

"I think you can safely leave Amy in Mrs Brett's capable hands and you can write to each other."

He turned to Amy

"Can you read and write, Amy?"

"Oh yes, Sir, Mrs Brett helped me." Amy said, proudly.

"Well I can't read nor write as I 'aven't never 'ad nobody to teach *me,* 'ave I?" Ned sounded close to tears.

"Is that all!" Edmund laughed. "You can be my first pupil. I need somebody to practice on so we can help each other. Is that settled then?"

"Yes!" they chorused.

"Ned, you come home with me. Mrs Dimlow has prepared a room for you at the Rectory. I think you will find it more comfortable than under the kitchen table! Just wait here while I go and say goodbye to the ladies."

When Edmund reported what had been arranged everyone was delighted for Ned.

"Amy will miss him." Amelia said.

"It may not be for long." Edmund said, enigmatically.

Once he had gone Amelia mused

"Do you think Edmund will offer Amy a post too?"

"That could be what is in his mind. We shall have to think about getting ourselves another maid." Mrs Trevise said.

"And *I* will go to the Domestic Agency this time, Madam!" Rose said, firmly.

"Yes, I think that would just as well, Rose dear. A mature woman would be best I think." Mrs Trevise agreed.

*****

Amelia and Edmund decided to get married in the Spring. The ladies were in a fever of preparation. Mrs Gipps planned on making a magnificent three-tier wedding cake. Rose made Amelia's wedding dress and honeymoon outfits. The drawing room at Springfield Road. seemed to be knee deep in silk of every colour from white to Amelia's favourite blue. Mrs Trevise, Rose, Mrs Kitson and Sophia plied their needles until their fingers ached and talked all the while. Lucy put herself in charge of bonnets, gloves and shoes and dragged Amelia round the West End until they were both exhausted. John complained that he never saw his wife and when he did all she could talk about was Amelia's wedding.

Amelia spent less and less time at the office and William was left to carry the bulk of the work. Amelia felt very guilty about this especially as it was nearing Christmas, their busiest time of year. When she apologized he said

"I enjoy it. After all, Aunt, I'll be in charge of the designing once you are married, won't I?"

Amelia had not considered this but now realized that her designing days were probably over. Seeing her sudden look of dismay and guessing the cause William said

"Of course I shall expect a great deal of help from you, Aunt. Don't think that just because you are buried in Herefordshire you can stop designing!"

"I shall be pleased to help you as much as I can, William, not that I think you really need it."

Edmund took his last Service as Vicar of St Mary's on Christmas Day. The next day he and Ned set off for Herefordshire. For several days afterwards Amy indulged in bouts of crying until Mrs Gipps could stand it no longer.

"Pull yourself together girl. There's a great deal of work to be done. You don't see Miss Wallace carrying on like that – she's got more dignity. Besides, what would your Ned think if he could see you?"

"Yes, Mrs Gipps. Thank you, Mrs Gipps." Amy sobbed.

Mrs Gipps shook her head and went back to decorating the Wedding Cake.

Rose, going into the kitchen on New Year's Eve to tell Amy to come into the drawing room to see in the New Year found her just about to put an ivy leaf into a dish of water.

"Whatever are you doing, Amy!"

"Well, if I put this leaf in 'ere and leave it for five days and if it's still green then it means that Ned will be safe and well for a 'ole year. But" she lowered her voice "if it goes funny it means 'e will 'ave misfortune and get sick."

Rose sighed. She doubted whether Amy would ever give up her superstitious habits and she resolved that she would keep an eye on the leaf and, if it showed any signs of being anything other than green, she would change it for a fresh one.

CHAPTER SIXTEEN

Ned was determined not to let either Amy or Edmund know how apprehensive he was about leaving London and everything that was familiar to him. He had never been into the 'country' which sounded as foreign as France. But it would be his first trip on a train and he couldn't wait. As he said goodbye to Amy the day before they left, he found it difficult to conceal his impatience to be off, especially as she was inclined to be tearful. In an attempt to cheer her up he said

"It won't be for long, Amy. The Guv. 'as got to come back soon to get married, and I'll write as soon as I'm able."

"Well, you see that you do, Ned Perkins!"

Was her reply accompanied by fresh tears.

"Of course. Nah I gotter go, the Guv's waitin."

Ned was up early the next day and after he had dressed he studied himself in the full-length mirror on the wardrobe door scarcely recognizing the young man who stared back at him. He had to admit he looked very smart in the new suit which Edmund had insisted on buying for him. Ned had objected that he didn't need 'charity' and Edmund told him that, since he was now his pupil, he had to be dressed properly and, in any case, he would be expected to work hard helping to get the house ready. Checking that he had left nothing behind he picked up his suitcase containing the rest of his new clothes and went down to the dining room where he consumed a hearty breakfast.

Ned had expected Edmund to have booked them third-class seats but when they arrived at the Railway Station he found Edmund had reserved a first-class compartment.

"All this space for us, Guv?" he asked in awe as he watched the Porter stow their luggage on the luggage rack.

"Of course, Ned." Edmund replied as he gave the Porter a generous tip.

"Cor!"

Ned settled into a seat by the window sighing contentedly. He watched London pass by, then open space followed by hills, fields, woods, rivers, lakes. He had never seen anything like it. It was ten times better than Hyde Park. The journey was long and tiring and Edmund slept most of the way but Ned could not tear himself away from the miles of country passing before his eyes and it was with great reluctance that he accompanied Edmund to the Dining Car, where Edmund watched in amusement as Ned calmly accepted the menu from the attendant, studied it carefully then confidently ordered the same as Edmund.

It was dark by the time they arrived at their destination where a carriage had been sent to meet them. By the time they arrived at the Manor House Ned was very tired and happy to go straight up to the room which had been prepared for him.

When he woke in the morning after a sound night's sleep he was surprised at how quiet it was. No shouting from the street vendors, no horse's hooves on the cobbles but only the sound of birds twittering. Eagerly getting out of bed he went to the window and looked out. There it was – the country. It was vast. He could see a large garden where several men were already working. Beyond the garden, fields where animals grazed and further still, woods. He could not wait to explore. Dressing quickly he left his room just as Edmund came out of his room further down the long corridor.

"Did you sleep well, Ned?"

"Yes, fank you, Guv. I'm going aht."

"Not this morning. After breakfast I want to tell you how I have arranged your work."

"O'course, sorry Guv. It's just that it's all so new."

"Yes, I know and you will have plenty of time to explore, never fear."

After a substantial breakfast, Edmund took him out into the garden where they walked up and down the gravel paths while Edmund outlined his plans for him.

"I should like you to help in the house in the mornings. Do you still have your old clothes?"

"Yes, Guv. I'm fond of 'em, like."

"Good. Wear those. Then, in the afternoons, you can wander where you like while I deal with Estate business."

"What abaht me readin'?"

"We will do that in the evenings. Are you agreeable to this arrangement?"

"Yes, Guv."

"Very well. Now go and change into your old clothes. You can start right away. No time like the present."

There was a great deal of work to be done as the house had not been lived in for many years and Ned worked very hard. The Estate Manager had recruited an army of women from the village to clean and scrub. Ned's job was to help move furniture and roll carpets. Most evenings were spent in the Library where Edmund gave him his reading and writing lessons. The shelves were filled with books of sermons which Ned found very dry and boring but once the new books which Edmund had ordered from London arrived he found the lessons more enjoyable and made good progress. He was determined to write to Amy as soon as possible and tell her all the wonders he had seen.

As Edmund had promised life was not all work and most afternoons while Edmund was closeted with his Estate Manager Ned was free to wander where he wished. After he had gone all over the house, which was larger than he had at first thought, he went out into the garden and spoke to the gardeners, asking them the names of the plants. He was particularly fascinated by the vegetable garden. He had never considered where vegetables came from, they just appeared on a costermonger's barrow, now he saw potatoes being dug out of the ground and strange looking plants growing up the garden walls which one of the gardeners informed him would bear peaches in the summer. There was a very dilapidated greenhouse which the elderly gardener he found there told him Mr Milton had ordered to be stocked with vines which would eventually yield grapes.

He was particularly interested in the horses as he had been a stable boy before he worked for the butcher. One of the stable lads called Reuben was very friendly and soon Ned was helping him with his work. As they worked they talked about their lives. Ned wanted to learn all about this place where he was going to make his home and Reuben was eager to hear about "that there Lunnon."

One morning as they were mucking out Reuben asked

"Would you like to come out shooting this afternoon? You could come home to tea with me after if you like."

"What are yer goin' to shoot?"

"Pigeons – they do be a nuisance. They can destroy a corn field."

Ned hesitated.

"Too soft are you? Too difficult for a Lunnoner is it?"

Reuben asked, scornfully.

"No, o'course not." Ned decided to make a clean breast of it.

"I've never bin shootin'".

Reuben stopped and leaned on his fork in astonishment.

"Well! If that don't beat all. Don't they have pigeons in Lunnon?"

"We don't shoot pigeons in London – only people."

"Sounds a funny kind of place. If you want to come I can teach you to shoot. There's nothing to it."

"All right then – I'll come. The Guv. don't need me this arternoon, 'es meetin' some Church geezer."

"And tea at my house after?"

"Yeah – that would be grand."

Ned enjoyed his afternoon especially as, under Reuben's expert tuition, he managed to bring down a bird.

"You take that one Ned – you shot it. Get my sister to put it in a pie. She makes a lovely pigeon pie does Martha."

"Martha our cook is yer sister?"

"Didn't you know your cook was my sister? Rev. Milton asked my mother if she knew anyone suitable and she said Martha would be happy to oblige. She wants to keep Martha here – Martha's always on about going down to Lunnon. Mother says Lunnon 'is not the place for a decent girl to work'. What is it really like?"

"It's all right. I ain't never lived nowhere else before. I fink I prefer 'ere now."

They had been walking down the village street as they talked and now came to a row of thatched cottages. Reuben stopped at the last one in the row where a woman was working in the neat front garden. She straightened up as Reuben opened the gate.

"There you be, Reuben. Hello, you must be Ned. I expect you're both ready for your tea."

"We are that, mother. Ned shot a pigeon."

"Did he – that's good."

"I told him to give it to our Martha to make a pie."

"Our Martha do make a very good pigeon pie. You and Mr Milton will enjoy it I know. Have you ever tasted pigeon pie, Ned."

"Not that I know of, Missis."

"Your mother never made you one then?"

"No." Ned said, shortly.

Reuben's mother glanced at his face but only said

"Do you come along in then."

They followed her into a small, neat kitchen where the table was laid with what looked to Ned like a feast for dozens.

"Sit down while I brew the tea. The little 'uns are off somewhere so they'll have theirs later."

Ned was hungry and immediately tucked in. Watching him wolf it down Reuben's mother asked

"Didn't they feed you in that old Lunnon?"

"Not like this, Missis. I'm always 'ungry 'ere."

"That's the clean country air. Nasty dirty place Lunnon so I be told. Don't know how anyone can live there. Martha said you was pale as death when you cum here. You've got some colour now, though."

Later, as he walked back to the Manor House Ned reflected on how much his life had changed in a month. He was learning to read and write and the Guv. had promised to help him write his first letter to Amy. He had made a friend and he enjoyed living in the country. The Guv. and Reuben's mother had been very kind to him and he wanted to repay them but could not think how.

The pigeon pie was a great success and Edmund congratulated him on his shooting skills.

"I can see we will not go hungry with you here, Ned."

For several days Ned turned the problem of a present for the Guv. and Reuben's mother over in his mind. He thought of asking Reuben but he wanted it to be a surprise. It must be something special. Something that could only have come from him.

He was out walking one fine afternoon when the solution literally leapt out at him in the shape of a small pig which stumbled through the hedge and landed at his feet. That was it – he would take this pig, which was just wandering about, butcher it and present the Guv. with the best cuts and Reuben's mother with the rest. He had butchered many a pig when the Butcher had a big order to fulfil and a bad hangover. He had no qualms about taking the animal. In London a loose pig would not last five minutes – finder's keepers. It was not his fault if the owner did not keep his pigs securely penned up. Capturing the pig was not difficult. Looking round he saw an abandoned outhouse and tied the animal inside while he searched for the necessary tools. By the late afternoon he had killed the pig, and cut it up into joints. He took the meat into the Manor House kitchen.

"Here's something for dinner tonight, Martha." he said as he laid the meat on the kitchen table.

Martha looked at him in surprise.

"Where did you get that?" she asked.

"Never mind where it cum from – can yer cook it really special?"

"Yes, of course I can."

"Don't say anything to the Guv. It's a surprise."

"Are you sure about this, Ned?"

"Yes, I am. Just cook it will yer."

Martha shrugged and turned back to her work. Ned left the kitchen and took the rest of the meat to Reuben's where he found only Reuben's younger brother at home. He made the boy promise to tell his mother that it was a present from Ned Perkins of the Manor House. As he walked home he felt like the Lord of the Manor.

Ned was at his place in the dining room early that evening.

"Hungry are you, Ned?"

"Yes, Guv."

"Here comes dinner now."

Martha carried in the dish preceded by a delicious aroma. She placed the dish in front of Edmund who took up the carving knife and fork.

"This looks very nice, Martha." he remarked as he began to carve.

"Thank you, Sir." Martha curtsied and withdrew.

"I didn't know we were slaughtering today." Edmund said as he placed a generous portion of meat and stuffing on Ned's plate.

Helping himself to potatoes Ned said

"It's a present, Guv."

"A present, from whom?"

"From me, Guv. A 'thank you' like."

"That's very nice of you, Ned but you shouldn't spend your money on me you know."

"Oh, it didn't cost me nothin'!"

Edmund very carefully put down the knife.

"Exactly *where* did this pig come from, Ned?"

He asked, quietly.

Ned began to feel uneasy. Something was wrong.

"Don't yer like pork, Guv.?"

"Yes, I enjoy a piece of pork, especially when it is so well prepared. I ask you again, Ned – where did you get this pig?"

"I wanted to get something for yer as yer've bin so kind to me but I 'ain't got much money. I was walkin' dahn the lane when this pig run aht in front of me."

"This pig?"

"Yes. I used to work for a Butcher so I know 'ow to slaughter and cut up meat. I thought yer would like it – a nice treat like."

Edmund sighed.

"Eat your dinner, Ned."

They ate in silence. Once they had finished Edmund got up.

"Come along, Ned."

Ned followed him to the Library and sat down at the table ready for his reading lesson. Edmund did not get out the reading books. Instead he sat at his desk.

"Come here, Ned."

Puzzled Ned got up and went and stood in front of the desk. His uneasiness grew.

"Tell me, Ned, if you saw a pig wandering around London what would you do?"

"I'd do what I did today – finders keepers – that's the Law, that is."

"It may be the law in London, although I doubt it, but you are in the country now. We do things differently. We look after each other. We help each other. We do not steal from each other. That pig belonged to somebody therefore you stole it – yes you did, Ned." As Ned went red and opened his mouth to protest. "In all probability that pig belonged to one of the cottagers who, in all likelihood, was saving it for some special family occasion – a Wedding or a Christening perhaps. Now you have deprived that family of the main part of their feast. I don't expect they can afford to slaughter another. What are you going to do about it, Ned?"

"ME!"

"Yes, you, Ned Perkins. I think you should find out to whom the pig belonged and offer to pay for it – not with money but with work. What do you say?"

"I don't see why – finders…"

"Ned, you stole somebody's pig. Now you must make restitution one way or the other, and you must *never* do anything like this again. Don't you see that if you are going to live here with me and help me run the School I must be able to trust you. A pig today – what will it be tomorrow? Are you ready to swear to me, on the Holy Bible, that you will never steal again?"

Ned stood in silence.

"I'm waiting, Ned. If you feel that you cannot so swear then I'm afraid I shall have no alternative but to send you back to London in disgrace."

Ned gulped. All his plans for himself and Amy in jeopardy and all over a stupid pig!

"What is your answer, Ned?"

Ned took a deep breath.

"I'll do it."

"Remember that you are swearing on the Holy Bible. If you forswear yourself you will be imperilling your immortal soul."

"I understand that, Guv. I won't never do nuffink like it again."

"Very well."

Edmund took up the large family Bible kept on his desk, and held it up.

"Put your right hand on the Holy Bible. Now say after me

'I, Ned Perkins, solemnly swear never to steal again.'"

Stretching out his hand and putting it palm down on the book Ned repeated the oath in a clear voice.

Edmund placed the Bible back on the desk.

"I want you to go out now and find the owner of that pig. I don't want to see you again until you can tell me you have done so."

"Yes, Mr Milton."

Ned felt confused, embarrassed and resentful. Then he thought of Amy. How ashamed of him she would be if she knew what he had done. She would never speak to him again. He suddenly realized that he could not bear the thought of losing Amy.

When he returned to the Manor House several hours later, tired and footsore, he went straight to the Library where he found Edmund at his desk, writing. Edmund looked up as he heard Ned enter the room. He did not smile.

"I've done it, Guv. I've found the pig's owner. It was one of the cottagers. 'E was real mad at first and give me a clip rahnd the ear. When I said I would work for 'im for nuffink 'e calmed dahn. Then 'e asked 'oo 'ad done the slaughterin'. 'E lives next door to Reuben and Reuben's mother asked 'im if 'e 'ad given 'er the meat. 'E said 'e could tell it 'ad bin done by somebody 'oo knew what they was doin'. I told 'im I did it and that I used to work for a Butcher in London, then 'e said 'e 'ad some more pigs to be slaughtered and I could do it. It would save 'im having to pay a Butcher."

Edmund smiled.

"Well done, Ned. I don't think it's too late for your lesson do you?"

"No, Guv. And Guv?"

"Yes, Ned."

"We don't 'ave to tell Amy abaht this, do we?"

"No, Ned we don't, it is just between you and me – and the pig's owner, of course!"

As Ned sat down at the table and picked up the book Edmund had placed there he resolved to learn more about the country and its unwritten laws.

*****

By the end of March all the preparations for Amelia's wedding were completed and the only topic of conversation was speculation regarding the weather.

"April is *so* changeable," Mrs Trevise worried.

"I don't think Amelia would care if there was thunder and lightning so long as she and Edmund could still get married." Mrs Kitson said.

"You don't think it possible there could be thunder do you, Anna?"

"No, of course not, Isabella. I'm sure the day will be beautiful."

Mrs Kitson's prediction proved to be correct. After a week of showers Amelia's Wedding Day dawned with clear skies and not a cloud in sight.

As Rose helped Amelia to dress she asked

"Are you happy, Amelia? This is really what you want? It's not too late to change your mind?"

"I'm very happy, Rose. But I shall miss you all very much."

"Don't forget that we are all coming to visit you in the Summer."

"That seems a long way away."

"It will soon pass. I expect you will be very busy getting the house and the school to rights. We shall be there before you know it. There – you look lovely, Amelia. Now I must go, the carriage will be waiting."

Rose gave her a quick hug and left the room before Amelia could see the tears in her eyes.

After the carriage had taken Rose and the other bridesmaids to Church Amelia came down the stairs to where John waited for her.

"You look – lovely, Amelia." He said.

"Thank you, John."

As she picked up her bouquet of white roses from the hall table he said

"I hope that you will be as happy with Edmund as I am with Lucy."

"I know I will be."

They left the house to get into Bert's hansom which, to Bert's delight, Amelia had insisted should take her the short distance to St. Mary's rather than the Hackney carriage John had wanted to hire.

The cab and Polly's harness were brightly polished and covered in white ribbons. On the driver's seat a beaming Bert sat dressed in his best suit and sporting a white favour while young Bert held the cab door open and helped them in. Once he had made sure they were comfortable he climbed up to sit next to Bert on the driver's seat.

At the Church Rose and the Bridesmaids were waiting in the Porch. Taking John's arm Amelia Wallace walked down the aisle to where Edmund and the Rev. Hendry waited. Twenty minutes later Amelia Milton retraced her steps arm in arm with her husband.

*****

At Springfield Road, Mrs Gipps was in the kitchen putting the finishing touches to the Wedding Feast while Amy and Ned prepared the dining room table.

"I do hope they don't meet a funeral on the way to the Church, Ned" Amy said, worriedly "that means an unhappy marriage."

Ned put down the glass he was polishing.

"Nah, you listen to me, woman, when we're married there'll be none of this superstitious nonsense. There ain't no sense in it."

"Do you want us to get married then, Ned?"

"Well o' course. Don't you?"

"Yes."

"Good. Me and the Guv. need a cook for the school and I reckon you'll do."

Mrs Gipps rushed into the room.

"Here they come – stir yourselves."

Soon the dining room was full of Amelia's family and friends. There were speeches and laughter and congratulations. The Wedding cake was cut and pronounced one of Mrs Gipp's triumphs.

Some time later Edmund attracted Amelia's attention where she stood talking to Rose

"I really think we should be going, Amelia. Trains don't wait even for newlyweds!"

"Yes, Edmund" Amelia meekly replied.

John, overhearing this exchange leaned towards Sophia saying "Amelia – tamed at last!"

But Sophia had seen the mischievous gleam in Amelia's eye.

CHAPTER SEVENTEEN

Amelia and Edmund had a loving but tempestuous marriage. They had four children, two girls and two boys. When Amelia had her first confinement Rose, true to her promise, came to look after her and stayed until the Doctor pronounced Amelia and the little girl brimming with health. For a while Amelia did the occasional design but her growing family and the school took up all her available time.

Edmund's school flourished, most of the pupils doing well. Some even entered the professions as Doctors, Teachers and Clergymen. In 1895 a separate school for girls was opened – one of the first in the country.

John and Lucy had no children but were very happy together.

Eleanor Jarrett recovered sufficiently to be allowed home and, when Patience died in 1890, she ran Arthur and his house very efficiently.

Mrs Trevise died in the flu epidemic of 1890. Mrs. Kitson and Rose continued to live at Springfield Road which Amelia rented out to them. When Mrs Kitson died in 1891 Rose decided to leave London. Amelia sold the house and Rose moved to a cottage on the Estate where she soon became a well-loved godmother to Amelia's children and courtesy Aunt to generations of the school's pupils who could always count on Aunt Rose when they were in trouble.

Amy and Ned married in 1889. On the day they were married Amy threw away all her good luck charms and never mentioned any superstitions again – at least not in Ned's hearing. They both worked on the Estate, living in the cottage next to Rose. They had twelve children, ten of whom survived infancy. Edmund took Ned's education in hand as he had promised and, in the course of time, Ned became a teacher at the school and Edmund's right hand.

When one of the farms on Edmund's Estate became vacant Amelia remembered Bert's dream of a little farm in the country and suggested that Edmund offer him the tenancy. Bert, his family and an ancient Polly moved to Herefordshire where Polly lived out her days giving occasional rides to the children and being thoroughly spoilt.

The Rev. Joseph Hendry married his Abigail, eventually becoming Bishop of Worcester.

The firm of Wallace, Douglass & Co. continued to prosper. When Mrs Kitson died she bequeathed the Company to John and upon John's retirement in 1905 William took over as Managing Director.